KING OF THE DAMNED

Ariel N. Anderson

KING OF THE DAMNED
ECHOES OF ETERNITY: BOOK 1

All rights reserved. No part of this book may be used or reproduced in any manner whatsoever without written permission except in the case of brief quotations embodied in critical articles or reviews.

The use of this publication in whole or in part to train generative artificial intelligence (AI) technologies is expressly prohibited.

This book is a work of fiction. Names, characters, businesses, organizations, places, events, and incidents either are the product of the author's imagination or are used fictitiously. Any resemblance to actual persons, living or dead, events, or locales is entirely coincidental.

All brand names and product names used in this book are trademarks, registered trademarks, or trade names of their respective holders. Ariel N. Anderson is not associated with any product or vendor in this book. All references to brand names and/or product names are used fictitiously.

Cover design by Rachel McEwan Designs
Graphic design by Book Covers by Melody
Character Art by Aedan Baez

eBook ISBN: 979-8-9882962-6-3
Paperback ISBN: 979-8-9882962-9-4

First Edition: April 2025

10 9 8 7 6 5 4 3 2 1

ARIEL N. ANDERSON

PROCEED WITH CAUTION

The Echoes of Eternity Duet is set in a fictional world with demons, monsters, witches, and magic. Themes of blood, sacrifice, and sex are prevalent throughout.

Content Warnings Include:

violence, near drowning, voyeurism, death, non-sexual degradation.

This book contains some explicit sexual content, including blood play and other adult themes intended for mature readers only.

A pronunciation guide can be found in the back of this book.

KING OF THE DAMNED

ARIEL N. ANDERSON

In Loving Memory of Anthony Sanchez

April 1979-November 2022

Your legacy is immortal.

National Suicide Prevention Lifeline:

1-800-273-8255

A small portion of the net royalties from all Ariel N. Anderson titles
are donated to the American Foundation for Suicide Prevention

KING OF THE DAMNED

ARIEL N. ANDERSON

"Their fangs get boners? Nice."

-My husband

KING OF THE DAMNED

Prologue
Kaius
1000 Years Ago

Monster. Abomination. Demon.

Those words swirl within my mind as I clutch my mother's lifeless body to my chest. I weep for her, the agony nearly too much to bear.

I'll never love again. Of that, I am certain.

I gave my heart so willingly. Trusted so thoroughly. I loved Yekaterina unconditionally, and it cost me everything. More than everything. My life, my family, my soul.

I was warned, and that's the part that leaves a bitter taste in my bloodstained mouth. It is known that the Ten Priestesses have a deceitful nature. They prey on men like me. They prey on their selfish desires, those same selfish desires that I foolishly shared with her.

Yekaterina cursed me, and it cost both of us our lives. It even cost the life of my innocent mother.

But souls live on, and as the witch's lifeless body turns to ash, the silver dagger I stabbed into her heart clatters to the ground. I feel her cold, black aura wrap around my spine, and I stiffen as her demonic voice enters my head, to tell me I will have but one chance to release her soul back into the world and break this wretched curse.

I vow at this moment that I will stop at nothing to end this immortal burden, stealing back my human life from the clutches of Yekaterina's wickedness.

But I will not bear this alone. I will create an army of my own. Worshippers of Yekaterina will become my slaves. The most cunning among Avrusa will become my allies.

I am Kaius Voroninov, King of Bloodlust, Betrayal, and the Damned, and all will share in this eternal torment with me.

One
Adelasia

This is my favorite part of the show. The anticipation that hits me right before I'm meant to perform. The way my hands tremble as I apply rouge to my cheeks. The way my legs feel weak as I put on my first costume of the night and tie the ribbons of my shoes.

So many women in this school would kill to be in my position. We've all worked so hard for this moment, and while I'm proud of myself for landing the lead role this season, there's an air of jealousy as the other ballerinas walk past me. I can see it in the little sneers on their faces that they each believe they deserved the role over each other and over me. It happens every season, and truthfully, when I'm in the corps, I look at the principal dancer with the same envy.

I stand at six feet tall–far taller than normal for a woman and certainly for a dancer. My height has come with its own set of challenges, the main one being that for many years, it was almost impossible to find a male partner that I didn't tower over. For much of my childhood, I simply was told to sit backstage, for my height was too much of a distraction. It was only by simple luck that eventually one of my male classmates hit a growth spurt.

That year, when I was sixteen, was the very first time I was allowed to participate in pas de deux class, and I never again wanted to let my height be a barrier to me. I practiced longer, trained harder, and took three times as many technique classes as anyone else. While I was not always the best, I certainly was one of the most determined, and it earned me respect that I did not have before.

The thing I love most about dancing is the freedom it gives me to be whoever I want. The freedom to be something as simple as a girl in love or something as majestic as a swan.

Tonight, I am to be a woman destined to fall in love with the moon, forced to watch it die every night only to return in the morning with no memory of me.

It's time for me to prove to everyone why I earned this role. As I regain my focus, the crowd goes silent, and the violinist begins to play a soft tune. My partner and I squeeze each other's hands in a small ritual of luck. The music begins to softly crescendo.

    I hold my breath in anticipation before fluttering out to the center of the town square in a romantic skirt. The light fabric dances with me as I tell a story of a vicious cycle of pain–not with words, but by making beautiful shapes with my body.

    I see my mother's proud gaze as she stands in the front row. Right before I exit the square for the next piece, I notice two sets of red eyes locked with mine. I quietly gasp and shake my head, convinced I'm just seeing things. After I blink, the red eyes are gone.

    Right. Seeing things.

    I bow to the crowd with my partner. The crystals of my skirt shimmer in the torchlight surrounding the town, radiating beautiful shades of orange and yellow from the white tulle.

    This costume, despite its beauty, comes with insecurity.

    I was born with a long, jagged, ugly scar down my spine. It would pass for a birthmark if the skin weren't raised and discolored from the rest of me. My parents tried everything to get rid of it. No potion or remedy the apothecary offered helped.

    We gave up after five years of painful treatment, and I eventually learned to live with the permanently blemished part of me.

Fortunately, since it's on my back, I tend to forget about it most days. Sometimes though, like when my ballet costume shows it...I envy the other girls in my school whose muscular, toned backs aren't soiled by the sight of a massive, grotesque scar down the entire length of their spines.

I take a deep breath as the music begins for my next number and I step out into the town center. The satisfying sound of my pointe shoes hitting the stone ground echoes off the buildings nearby as I leap and turn. At the end of my number, I raise tall in a tight first position, my arms delicately poised above my head.

The applause begins before the music ends, and in a truly dramatic beginning to what I guess is the worst night of my life, the torches lighting the town center burn out. The crowd gasps in confusion.

Two sets of malicious red eyes appear in front of me, and they don't even bother to cover my mouth to hide my scream.

Two
Kaius

The night is cool, a recent storm leaving the ground damp and the sky covered in thick gray clouds. These nights have always been my favorite.

The way the grass smelled so fresh, and how my home was always a bit cooler after a hot summer day. The first sip of crisp water from the basin. When I was a boy, the hours after a thunderstorm were always serene.

I swirl the thin layer of remaining blood-spiked wine around my silver goblet before bringing it to my lips. I stare out to the horizon, past the jagged rocks that rise high above the valley, towards the East.

I have done this every morning for centuries. I stand here in the hours before the sun crests over the valley, hoping that this will be the day the caress of the sun doesn't burn my skin.

I've never had such luck.

My people know not to disturb me in these hours. It's not forbidden, but the last person to do so ended up as ashes on the balcony, left to die in the dreaded sunlight.

Recognizing footsteps is a skill I've become far too good at. Though I can see perfectly fine in the dark, I've learned to rely on my other senses just as much as my sight. A keen ear sometimes reveals more than a keen eye.

It's Dravon approaching. My long-standing ally. My right hand. Someone I trust.

"Dangerous game you're playing this morning," I murmur, only half-joking.

"Two worms in the prisons are requesting you meet them there. They claim it's a matter of some urgency," Dravon says, and I can hear the disgusted curl of his lip when he mumbles something about not being a messenger boy.

I tilt my chin in acknowledgment but don't move my gaze from the horizon.

"They had a human with them," Dravon adds as he steps to my side. "A tall, thin thing. I did not see her face, but she smelled–" an exhale of breath "–*divine.*"

I raise a brow. "They want an audience with me for new livestock?"

"Curiously, they were requesting livestock in reward."

Finally, I let my eyes drift to the man at my side. I hand Dravon my goblet, and for the first time in nine hundred years, I turn my back to the sunrise.

Three
Kaius

  The cattle cells smell of human waste and death. The mortals foolish enough to wander into vampire territory are captured and kept here until either they die or are claimed by one of my kind.

  For some humans, to be claimed is the hope. Being kept as a blood slave has been fetishized, especially amongst those who have no roof over their heads or no food in their bellies.

  Vampires keep their cattle well-fed. Malnourished blood leaves a foul aftertaste. Healthy blood is sweet, like fresh fruit, and savory, like slow-roasted meat.

Not that I can remember what those things taste like.

It's been so long since I've tasted anything other than blood and wine. Sometimes I gaze at the human food in the kitchens, and as I do, my mouth salivates with the ghostly memory of a ripe berry or a well-seasoned duck.

I've spent the last millennium longing for the things I took for granted as a human, and the only reason I'm in this fetid dungeon is because, for the first time in all these years, there's hope that I can have them back.

The air grows more stale with each silent step I take deeper into the tunnels. I can hear whispers echoing off the walls, but more importantly, I can hear the panicked flutter of an unwillingly captive human's heart.

I hear a small whimper and the clank of human bones bouncing off the thick iron bars of the cells. I stick to the dark and pause behind a corner to watch two sallow, greasy vampires accost a woman in the cell.

Her bright blue eyes stare up at them filled with pure terror, made even more evident by the smell of fear in her blood. They have her arm in a tight grip, pulling her into the cell door and mocking her whimper with their own.

"What do ya' think?" one asks the other, sniffing the inside of the woman's wrist as the other licks his teeth. "Should we have a taste before Lord Kaius arrives?" He smells her wrist again and makes a noise of awe. "She smells delicious."

The second vampire smacks away his hand, causing him to release the woman. She falls to the floor and backs away into her cell until I can no longer see her from where I watch them. "You know how the Dread Lord feels about sharing his treasures. I have no desire to find myself on the receiving end of his wrath, and if you were smart, you'd be inclined to feel the same."

The first man mutters to himself, and both stiffen and bow when I reveal myself from the shadows.

Air seems to fill my petrified lungs when I get a better look at the woman in the cell. She's wearing a dancer's dress. White. Delicate chiffon draping over her long legs.

Her eyes are so vibrantly blue, even in the dim light, and even brimmed with tears and redness. It's almost…violent in the most stunning way. Like I could stare right through them and see not only her soul, but my own reflected.

"Lord Kaius," one of the worms says, pulling my attention from the woman, "We humbly ask for your favor in exchange for this gift," he finishes, with a grand and over-exaggerated bow.

I turn my nose up in disgust, shifting my gaze to the girl. "I have no need for more cattle. You dare summon me to this decrepit prison for a stupid human?"

They look at each other and smile. "This one's special." The shorter of the two suddenly bangs the iron bars, causing the girl to gasp and curl into a ball. "You there! Turn around!" She doesn't move, so he reaches through the bars and grabs her wrist. "I said turn around," he repeats, before shoving her, and she hunches herself over her knees with her back to us.

The two worms resume their snickering because they know her value—or at the very least, they've heard whispers of the value of a single scar. "We want twenty cattle of our choosing, to do as we please."

"Done," I reply. "Has anyone else seen this human?"

"No, sire. We brought her straight here."

"Where did you find her?"

"Just beyond the valley, in the town of Lemory. We was huntin' for some fresh meat. Saw her dancin' in the plaza for one of them full moon celebrations the humans do." He laughs. "Snatched her right from the courtyard in front'a all of 'em. Squealed like a pig, she did."

I let silence fill the air for a moment, and then I reach into the chests of my two subjects, grabbing their hearts and ripping them out. Their bodies fall to the floor with a thud before turning to ash.

The human girl watches me drop the hearts at my feet before I take a handkerchief from my pocket and wipe my hands clean. She gulps slowly, as if trying to swallow bile creeping up her throat.

With a curl of my lip and a huff, I turn from her, stepping over the remaining ashes with every intent to leave this prison and her in it.

But then she softly croaks, *'wait'*, and something deep in the very center of my being compels me to stop.

And in this singular moment, the entirety of my world shifts.

I just don't know it yet.

Four
Adelasia

"Wait!" I say quietly, but frantically. He turns, staring back at me almost with the same bewilderment as I have.

He's taller than anyone I've ever seen. The top of his head hitting just below the top of the cell door. His silver-toned white hair is halfway tied back and falls just above his shoulders. He's wearing a pitch-black tunic and an equally dark cape. It hangs over his shoulders and brushes the floor slightly. The light from the single fire outside my cell reveals that the material looks to be raven or crow feathers. They bellow slightly from the draft in the hallway.

"What is your name?" he asks.

The question makes me stiff, but maybe this tiny shred of humanity he's showing by asking my name is the only saving grace I have to cling to. Carefully, I crawl to the iron door. I grip the bars and pull myself up slightly. I give him a pleading look and something in his chiseled face softens as he squats down to be closer in height to me.

"Please let me out," I beg.

"Your name," he replies. *Not a question this time.*

"Adelasia," I tell him.

"Adelasia," he repeats slowly, as if to savor all four syllables. His glowing red eyes flicker to mine. "Are you hurt?"

I shake my head. "No."

He nods curtly and then moves to stand up. My hand reaches out to grab the edge of his cape, afraid he's going to leave me in here to die and rot. There's another man across from me in a different cell, and he looks to be in horrible shape. Malnourished. Covered in dirt and his excrement. I don't want that to be me.

This vampire, *Kaius*, pauses mid-squat and eyes me with curiosity.

"Please," I beg. "Please don't leave me here."

"Do you know why they took you, Adelasia?"

I shudder. "So you can...*feed*?"

He laughs quietly to himself as if I've just told him a joke. "No. That's not why you're here at all." He fully stands and with minimal effort, he grips the iron bars of my cell door and rips the entire thing off its hinges. The door falls to the ground with a loud clang. He removes his cape and holds it out for me. "Come. Quickly."

"Where are you taking me?"

"Does it matter? You asked me to let you out of your cage and that's what I've done."

"Are you going to kill me?"

"The probability of that grows every second you keep me waiting here. *Stand up.*"

I do as he says and stand. I dust off my skirt before letting him wrap the cloak around my shoulders. It's warm. Much warmer than I imagined feathers would be, and it smells...spicy in the best way. Though I'm tall, I'm nothing compared to him, and the cloak bunches around my ankles.

He grabs me by the wrist and pulls me along with him. He leads me out of the small prison, and we emerge from underground, allowing me my first glimpse of the mysterious vampire settlement. The demons of the night have always kept to themselves here. I suppose the tall ridges of the valley provide some protection from both the sun and demon hunters.

I never expected the city to be so...civilized. I suppose I imagined corpses and skeletons. Feral vampires that hiss as we pass. Blood spatter and gore littering the streets.

But much to my surprise, the buildings are unlike anything I've ever seen, erected out of the ground in thick, black marble structures that are ornate and beautiful. Gold, silver, and copper inlays make the sunlight that hasn't quite crested over the jagged valley glimmer off the buildings, masking them in a pretty glow.

The man pulling me seems unconcerned with the impending sunlight.

The pavement is perfectly aligned charcoal gray stone. The street lamps are intricate wrought iron.

After only a short walk, a massive marble palace appears in front of us. It's directly in the center of the settlement and the biggest structure I've ever seen.

It's a beautiful, gothic masterpiece, but there's something sinister about it. Something unholy and corrupted. I may no longer be in that cell, but I am still a prisoner.

I gulp, swallowing the burning, aching lump in my throat. Kaius leads me leisurely through the palace, straight to a bedroom. It's large but filled with uneasy emptiness. The only furniture in the room is a small bed in the center, pushed against a blank wall.

No lights. No trinkets. No paintings. Nothing more than a single pillow on the bed and cold loneliness. There isn't even a quilt.

Kaius finally releases my wrist, and I immediately put distance between us. It's so dark here that I can only see the glow of his red eyes. My stomach drops when I notice him taking a step closer to me. And then another and another until I'm flat against a cold marble wall.

"Turn around."

I don't. Instead, I whimper.

I hear him sigh. "Let me be clear, little human girl: I am not known for my patience. If I need to ask twice, I won't be asking. I'll be *taking*."

He roughly grabs my arms and twists me so I'm now facing the wall. He removes the cloak from my shoulders, and I'm instantly shivering from both fear and how painfully cold it is. So cold that my bones ache and my toes are numb.

He rips the fabric of my costume down my back, and I begin to sob as his fingers trace down the length of my spine, right over my scar. It's still pitch-black in the room, so he must be able to see in the dark.

I wonder how clearly he can see the tears dripping down my cheeks.

"This mark—where did you get it?"

Sniffling, I tell him the truth. "I was born with it."

"And how old are you?"

"Twenty-seven."

"*Twenty-seven*," he repeats, almost sounding disgusted.

I feel him step away, and his footsteps recede until he leaves the room, and the door gently closes behind him. The distinct sound of a lock clicks in place.

He didn't even leave me with a light.

Several long hours pass, and I make it through them by thinking of home—of my friends—of dance. I can't imagine what it was like for my mother to watch me get taken right in front of her eyes by two monsters.

I'm so cold I think I've permanently turned a shade of blue. Kaius left his cloak draped over the bed. I found it as I was feeling around for anything to use as a weapon, a lockpick, anything to help me out of this predicament.

I found nothing.

So instead, I curled up into a ball and used the cloak as my only source of warmth.

I don't know exactly how long it's been, but judging by how tired and hungry I am, I guess that it's probably what I would consider dinnertime. I've been in this bedroom since dawn, but I have no way of knowing if the sun is still up because there are no windows.

The door opens, and the groan of the heavy metal sits like a rock in my gut. Red eyes stand tall in the doorway and stare at me as I cower behind the cloak for some semblance of protection.

He steps closer. My heart begins to beat wildly in my chest and in the dark, I once again feel around for anything I can use as a weapon. There's nothing, but the door is open.

Can I really outrun a vampire? Most likely not, but I have to try. He finally reaches me, and I feel his cold hands grip my shoulders to pull me to my feet.

I do the only thing I can do. I lift my hand and smack him across the cheek. I think I've startled him, because he lets me go, and I run. I run for my life. I run as fast as my legs can carry me.

But when I reach the first turn at the end of the hall, I run into a cold chest and instantly, the braziers along the corridor light themselves, allowing me to see Kaius standing in front of me with a wicked grin on his face.

He grabs my arms again and pins them to my sides. I struggle against his grasp, but then dense red magic wraps around my body, holding me completely still. I shudder when he brushes my messy hair out of the way and nuzzles into my neck as he inhales deeply. "Careful, Adelasia." I feel a slight prick in my skin and then his tongue licks along the column of my throat until he reaches my ear before he sensually whispers, *"Fear makes your blood taste better."*

Five
Kaius

And it was...*delicious*. Perfectly sweet with the sour tang of fear on the aftertaste. I like it when they struggle. It makes for a more satisfying meal.

This girl isn't like the other humans kept prisoner in the walls of my palace, to be kept as cattle and feasted on at the leisure of myself or my court. This human isn't for consumption. She's the key to undoing this wretched curse that was thrust upon me one thousand years ago. This agony I've endured for a millennium is all but over.

All I must do is protect her until the next full moon, when magic will be the strongest. Every curse bestowed by a Priestess begins and ends on a full moon. There is something inherently tragic in that—how one of the most beautiful things in the night can be marred by dark magic.

I have no way of knowing what breaking this curse means for the rest of the vampire race. It could cure only myself, or it could cure every vampire in the world.

If word gets out about who Adelasia is and her role in breaking the curse, lesser vampires who also wish to be cured may not be willing to gamble on it and attempt to take her from me.

I refuse to let that happen. I've waited too long and lost too much to lose it all now.

When the human told me her age, I was shocked. She's been under my nose for nearly three decades and by chance, she's found by two loyal subjects willing to give me whatever I desire in exchange for just a drop of my favor. I appreciate their loyalty, but it was better that I remove them from the equation, lest they open their mouths around the wrong ears.

Yekaterina, the Priestess who condemned me to this life was beautiful in her wickedness. It was the reason I fell in love with her so deeply. She was the same kind of relentless evil that I myself was all that time ago. She and I lived for the torment we inflicted on others because it brought us pleasure.

It was all a ruse. *All of it*. The years I spent falling carelessly in love with that beautiful creature, one of the most powerful beings in the world, came with a consequence I never could have fathomed: deception.

Yekaterina didn't love me. Cursing me with bloodlust and immortality was her cruel way of ending things between us when she grew tired of me. In my rage, I ripped out her spine, and her nine sister Priestesses only cursed me further for it.

I was wild with anger in the beginning and created other vampires just to be cruel. But a millennium of loneliness has a way of putting things into perspective. I'm not the same beast I was a thousand years ago.

I hate Yekaterina for what she did to me, but that change in perspective is why I think I'm feeling...*hesitation* about what I have planned for Adelasia.

Perhaps I've grown soft for the finality of a mortal life—knowing it's what I've been chasing for so long. I always thought I'd do what needed to be done without a second thought, but that's because I always assumed this curse breaker would be more like the wicked soul that has intertwined itself with hers.

I do not know Adelasia, nor do I wish to, but she is not Yekaterina, and someday soon I will have to face the reality that my freedom comes at the expense of an innocent.

As she stands here, trapped by my magic with a single drop of her sweet blood running down her neck, pooling at her collarbone, I feel guilty. When I see the slight blue tint of her milky skin, I feel worse.

She's cold. Freezing, even. She keeps looking at the braziers lining the corridor as if she's considering jumping into one for warmth.

This human girl may be a means to an end, but for the time being, she is my guest. I shall be a good host.

I free her from her magic bonds. Adelasia feels at her neck where her blood drips down from her wound. She grows a shade paler when she sees it smeared across her fingers. Her eyes flicker to me as if to examine my reaction, but my face is cold as stone.

I raise her chin with the knuckle on my forefinger. She cowers slightly but has the good sense to stay put. Running is futile in her situation. Even if she did manage to escape this palace, five miles of vampire territory lay between her and her little human world. She wouldn't make it five *steps*, let alone miles.

"Come," I command. She hesitantly follows as I lead her back to her room and into the adjacent bathing chamber. I mindlessly wave my fingers and the bath fills with hot, steaming water. I turn to her and gesture to it with an open hand.

"When you're done, I will take you to the dining room for supper."

"I...don't have any clothes," she whispers with a flush to her cheeks, her eyes flickering down to her torn, dirty costume and then back up to me.

I wave my fingers again and one of my dark gray tunics appears on the black marble countertop. "Tomorrow we'll find something more suitable for you to wear."

Adelasia blinks as if trying to pull herself out of a trance. "Tomorrow?"

"The day that follows this one."

She makes a noise of frustration. "I know what tomorrow means."

I understand. She didn't expect it to make it past the night. The notion of '*tomorrow*' seems foreign and impossible to her.

I take a step towards her and grip her shoulders before licking the lone drop of blood remaining on her collarbone. I take a deep breath of satisfaction and simply whisper, "*Tomorrow*," into her ear before stepping out of the bathing chamber.

It takes her an irritatingly long time to clean herself. I can hear her rustling around the room, searching for a way out or a weapon. I applaud her determination, but I am not stupid. Anything she can think of, I have already considered.

I pace around the bedroom while I wait. My blood thrums with the exhilaration of knowing that my immortal prison will be a memory in just a few short weeks.

When Adelasia emerges from the bathing chamber, her raven-black hair is still dripping wet. The moisture soaks into the thin fabric of my tunic, long locks falling over her shoulders and breasts. Though I see nothing improper, she notices my stare and crosses her arms over her chest.

I place my hand on the small of her back and gently push her towards the door, guiding her through the halls until we reach the dining room. I feel the tension in her fading slightly when she sees an array of human food arranged on the table.

Cheeses and fruits, breads and heavily seasoned chicken. A pitcher of filtered water and a golden decanter of red wine. Roasted vegetables soaking in lemon butter. A small tray of shortbread cookies topped with raspberries.

"You're surprised," I say as she stares at the food. "You're not the only human in this palace, Adelasia. We like to keep the mortals well-fed. Nothing tastes worse than malnourished blood."

I look at her, and she seems sickened by that knowledge.

Good. Her clear disdain for my way of life will make ripping her apart so much more satisfying.

I suppose that guilt I was feeling washed away with her bath.

I take a seat at the head of the table where a single goblet rests for me. On my left sits a full place setting with a napkin and silver utensils for her.

I gesture to the chair and she tentatively sits. I pour myself a glass of wine from one decanter and offer to fill her own goblet from another. Her face twists with disgust. "Don't be dramatic. It's *wine*."

She sits quietly for a few minutes. I can hear her stomach gurgling and eventually, her hunger outweighs her hesitation. She fills her plate with a pitiful slice of chicken and a small scoop of roasted vegetables. She takes tiny sips of water in between equally tiny bites until her plate is empty.

I sip my own wine and watch inquisitively as she stares at the chicken resting on the serving dish. My eyes move to the meat and then back to her, where she seems to be fidgeting and more nervous than she was a moment before.

She blinks rapidly as if hiding tears, takes a deep breath, and sits stiffly back in her chair without meeting my eyes. I lean forward a bit, resting my forearms on the table and clasping my hands together in curiosity.

"*Don't be foolish*," I warn. She looks at me then, and I can hear the way her fingers tighten around the knife she's tried to sneak into her lap without me noticing. She swallows and carefully sets it back on the table.

I sit back in my own chair, nursing my blood-spiked wine. I don't particularly like it—I prefer it fresh—but it's one of the things that makes me feel mortal again, and spiking it is the only way my body can consume liquids without rejecting them entirely.

It's also a way to keep the humans in line, particularly the cattle. They fear becoming our next delicacy.

As Adelasia stares forward, I examine her face. The warmth from the hearth has helped some of the natural color return to her cheeks and lips. She's no longer shivering, and her hair has begun to dry. The more nervous she becomes, the more prominent the vein running down her jugular entices me. The one taste of her blood was nowhere near enough, and I find myself craving it more than usual. Not blood, but *her* blood. My teeth begin to ache as I think about it more and more.

Just one taste...

In the tense moment of silence between us, while I'm lost in the quickly growing bloodlust, Adelasia jolts up from her seat before taking her dinner knife and plunging it into my chest.

I look down at the knife and grunt as I remove it. There's a thick layer of blood gathered on the blade. I stare at her as I lick the silver clean, and then smile in a way that has my fangs on full display.

I whisper to her a single word:

"*Run.*"

Six
Adelasia

He tells me to run.

So I do.

I fuel myself with desperation instead of fear as I sprint through the halls. I don't even know where I'm going. I don't know if there are other vampires lurking here. I reach a dead-end wall, and when I turn to run back the other way, my blood runs cold with pure, unfiltered terror.

Kaius is standing at the opposite end of the hall. The front of his dark tunic is wet from where his blood seeps through the fabric.

And his eyes–his eyes are pure black, with black and red veins pouring out from the sockets. His fangs are longer, his body is poised like a predator.

This is the demon we humans fear. The face of nightmares.

He walks towards me. Each step is slow but purposeful. As he passes the braziers lining the walls, they come alight with blue fire to match the cold fury in his eyes.

Those depthless, unholy eyes.

When he reaches me, I've forgotten how to breathe. He stands tall, beautiful, and deadly, mere inches from me.

"I warned you not to be foolish," he says, before leaning into me, trapping me between the wall and his body. He inhales deeply at the curve of my neck. "What should be your punishment for such...disobedience?"

I shiver as I feel his fangs drag along my throat, though not enough to break the skin. He's testing me. Intimidating me. Daring me to move.

"Please..."

He purrs into my neck. "Answer the question, Adelasia, before I rip out your throat."

"Please. I'm sorry. I'll do anything, just please don't hurt me," I beg, putting my hands against his chest to try and push him away. My chest heaves faster and faster with the anxiety and panic growing within me.

"*Anything*, hm?" he exhales a snort. "What could a human *possibly* offer me?"

"I'll–I'll–I'll dance for you."

Instantly, the braziers in the hall return to a normal, orange glow and his eyes return to their normal red hue as he reels back to look at me.

"Explain."

"I...um..." I struggle to form words, somehow even more uneasy now than I was when he was poised at my neck. "I can dance for you. It's my life. I don't have any skills or experiences outside of ballet. I...I could entertain you and your court?" I give him a defeated sigh when his face shows no emotion at my proposal. "That's all I have."

He contemplates in silence for a moment, and I watch as his eyes trace down my face to my neck then back up again.

"I shall allow you a suite of your own and protection from the other vampires here in exchange for three things. One, you may not leave this palace without an escort—meaning *me*. Two, you will keep yourself modest and covered at all times."

I look down, ashamed. I understand what he means. He finds my scar grotesque just as everyone else does, and does not wish to see it again.

"Three, you shall dance for me, and only me, during your time here."

I swallow. "And...how long will that be?"

In response, he simply gives me a sneer and an upturn of his chin before walking away, taking the light of the braziers with him.

Our deal sits heavy in my gut like a rock as I dress. It's been two days since I've seen Kaius. True to his word, not one vampire has bothered me. I've seen not one soul. My meals are delivered to my room, and the one who delivers them is always gone before I open the door, even if I open it as soon as I hear a knock.

I've had no courage to leave my suite yet.

Yesterday when I woke, the wardrobe was filled with clothing: ornate and beautiful dresses, nightgowns and robes, leotards and tights, trousers and tunics and corsets. Shoes and underthings. Anything I could possibly wish to dress in is freely available to me, including a deep red ballet costume with a tutu decorated in delicately sewn lace and magnificent crystals.

I supposed that costume was meant to be worn as I danced for him tonight as part of our arrangement. I have no intention of humoring this man with dazzling costumes. He stole me from my home. If I have to dance to survive, then I will, but I won't embellish it with costumes and smiles to make him feel better about himself for what he's done to me.

Instead, I've chosen to wear a simple black leotard with a turtleneck and long sleeves, with a long romantic skirt in a shade of deep purple tulle.

When I arrive in the main hall, where Kaius requested I meet him, he's sitting on his throne atop a raised platform. A staircase of four narrow black marble steps is all that separates us when I come to a stop. His white hair glows a soft shade of yellow from the braziers that line the room. In his hand is a silver goblet. When he takes a sip, his lips are tinted deep red, and that tells me all I need to know about what's in that goblet before he licks it away with his tongue.

He silently lets his gaze travel down my body, though the gesture doesn't make me uncomfortable. I'm used to others looking at me with critical eyes, always looking for a hair out of place, a sliver of weight gain, or a run in my tights.

Everyone has always been so determined to find a flaw in me when all I've ever wanted to do is dance.

"Your hair," he says, causing me to subconsciously touch the bun at the base of my skull.

"What about my hair?"

"Take it down."

"Why?" I ask, utterly confused.

"I'd like you to let your hair free." I give him a look of irritation. He sighs and rolls his eyes. "I'd like to see you unbound. Not so rigid and perfect."

"It's not about rigidity," I spit. "It's precision. If you wished to see something more sensual and wild, then perhaps you should have kidnapped a different dancer."

He chuckles. "I am not the one who kidnapped you."

"And yet you're now my captor."

"Captors don't let their captives roam freely," he replies curtly. "Though if you don't appreciate that freedom, perhaps you'd prefer I treat you as a bitch on a leash?"

He conjures exactly that around my throat, tugging it hard enough to force me to fall to my knees. He gives me a sardonic laugh before he makes it disappear.

"I'm not an animal!" I say through gritted teeth as I stand again. I will not allow this man the pleasure of seeing me on my knees in front of him.

"You're a human."

"So?"

"I see no difference," he quips, his chin raised in challenge. My mouth falls open in shock. "Do you know what we call the silly humans that wander into our stronghold? The ones we keep for ourselves to feed on?"

He pauses, but I say nothing, and his mouth twists upward into a wicked sneer, showing off his fangs. "Cattle."

Furious, I stomp up the narrow staircase. My dance shoes make loud clacks against the marble as I do. When I reach him atop the platform, I raise a hand and smack him as hard as I can. So hard that my wrist and palm hurt after the impact. "You're a monster," I mutter in disgust.

He smiles again before sipping his wine. "Little girls should be scared of monsters."

I slap the goblet downward, spilling its contents over the front of his gray tunic. "I'm not a little girl, and I'm certainly worth more than livestock."

Once again, he flashes his dangerous teeth. "*Prove it* and dance, or I shall throw you in with the other cattle and let my coven rip you to shreds."

Calling his bluff, I ask, "If I'm so expendable, why didn't you do that in the first place? Why waste your time filling my belly and my wardrobe if you'd rather exsanguinate me?"

This time, instead of smiling, he grinds his teeth as he stares up at me. He stands so quickly that I nearly lose my footing and tumble down the steps. He roughly grabs me by the elbow and drags me out of the throne room, to an adjacent smaller room where a few vampires sit huddled around a table, drinking and laughing. Their merriment ceases when Kaius and I enter the room.

Without so much as a glance in my direction, he addresses the men.

"Gentlemen…" He raises his eyebrows in amusement before shoving me further into the room. "Enjoy your dinner."

The second the door slams shut and I hear it lock from the outside, I go into pure survival mode. Screaming, crying, running, cowering. Once they corner me, they take turns playfully lunging at me–toying with me–snickering at my fear and my feeble attempts to scratch and hit them.

One grabs me, and that's when I stop fighting and start begging. As the vampire inhales the scent of my neck deeply, I scream, "*Please!*"

As soon as the word leaves my mouth, the door opens, and Kaius steps back into the room. At his reappearance, the vampire lets me go, and the others clear a path for him to approach me. As he does, he holds out a hand, tenderly, as a lover would do.

With my pride and stubborn defiance gone, I take it. His fingers wrap around my palm with the softest care, and he walks with me in silence until we reach my room. My eyes are still leaking tears, my body still trembling in fear. He lets go of my hand and then reaches up to let my hair out of its bun. He gently runs his fingers through the locks until they're draped around my shoulders, and then he lifts my chin with his thumb and forefinger.

"I told you, Adelasia. I don't ask twice," he whispers, before using whatever magic he possesses to put out the fires keeping my room lit and warm, and gently closes the door behind him.

Once again locking me in like the animal he believes I am.

Seven
Adelasia

In the morning, breakfast is delivered to my room. I quietly stoke the fading flame in the fireplace as I sit on the floor and nibble on some bread with jam. I bathe, and as my hair drips cold water around my feet, I emotionlessly dress in a leotard and tights.

After I lace up the ribbons of my dancing shoes, I use the vanity chair as a barre as I leisurely warm up my muscles and soothe the chill in my bones.

When I rise on my toes to spin and warm up the left side of my body, I find Kaius standing at the entrance to my room. He's eerily quiet. Uncomfortably still. Maliciously cold. His raven feather cloak sits heavy and luxurious on his tall frame. His silvery-white hair is loose around his face. Something about him looks troubled.

I swallow. "What do you want?"

"I came to ask you what you knew about vampires."

I scoff. "My opinion on demons like you shouldn't be any of your concern."

In truth, I know very little about vampires and other monsters of the world. All of my knowledge comes from legends and tales from the few survivors that have been passed down through generations.

The Nine Priestesses, the keepers of magic and defenders of the darkest corners of the world are said to be responsible for all demons.

After vampires were created, the werebeasts came next; shapeshifters that favor the instincts of predators—wolves, bears, leopards, hawks. The werebeasts often prefer their animal form over their human form, and many give up their human troubles in favor of living amongst each other in the wilds.

With each new creation, the monsters became more wicked and vile until the world was crawling with horrors beyond imagination. Walking corpses. Giant spiders. Krakens of the deep so vicious that the oceans have been reclaimed, and no human has dared cross the Endless Sea in nearly six hundred years.

There were once ten Priestesses, but our human legends only go as far as to say one simply vanished without a trace, and that shortly after she disappeared, hordes of vampires took her place and quickly became the apex predator.

Kaius grits his teeth, but to my shock, he doesn't retaliate with violence or try to subdue me with fear. He steps further into the room and takes a seat in a chair set up near the fireplace.

I turn my back to him and continue my technique warm-up. I can feel him staring at me, and his gaze is as cold as this strange palace. As that unsettling thought crosses my mind, my mood sours further when I realize why my dancing feels so lifeless.

I miss music. I miss the beautiful crescendo of the orchestra and the delicate scale of the piano accompanying my steps. I miss the way the music echoes off the floors as my dance shoes do.

With a huff, I stand up straight and eye the black marble wall in front of me with annoyance. No windows, no music, no warmth.

Yet he has the nerve to call *me* the animal.

"What is it?" Kaius asks from behind me. I turn to face him with my hands on my narrow hips. He's flipping a silver dagger between his fingers. It does not leave cuts across his skin.

Why carry a weapon that cannot harm vampires in a vampire settlement?

"This place. It's lifeless." To add venom to my words, I raise my eyebrows in challenge. "Like you."

"Trust me, Adelasia, I have plenty of life left in me. I cannot say the same for you, as you insist on testing my patience."

I huff. "You want me to dance as a way to beg for my life? Fine. The least you could do is not force me to do it in silence."

His face falls from bitter amusement to anger. "Perhaps I've spent my lifetimes doing things more important than being polite to crass humans and filling their ears with music."

As he finishes his sentence, he lunges for me and takes my wrist in his large hand. He examines the skin of my inner wrist as I whimper from the tightness of his hold.

A ruby the size of my palm dangles from an ornate silver chain around his neck, and it begins to glow a brighter shade of red and hum softly. When it stops, I feel a sting at my wrist and jerk my hand free from his grasp. I clutch it to my chest as the pain subsides and then examine the area.

A small, red, eight-pointed star now mars the delicate milky skin of my wrist.

"What is this?" I ask in a panic. "What have you done to me?"

"If you want music, make your own, Adelasia."

"What?"

"It's magic," he growls, frustrated. "You want music? Light? Warmth? Make it yourself. I'm not your servant."

"You're right, you're my warden."

"You have two minutes to dance, or I'll rip out your throat."

"Then do it!" I shout. "Stop filling my head with empty threats. You've already taken me away from everything I loved." I don't mean to, but my voice begins to quiver. "If you're going to kill me or feed on me then just be the monster you want me to believe you are, and do it."

He stares down at me with a completely blank expression on his face, but something in those bright red eyes seems...disappointed.

"What do you know about vampires?" he asks again, carefully enunciating each word as if he believes I'm slow. My silence displeases him, and he shakes me. "Tell me!"

The anger in his voice combined with the way he shouted it has my resolve cracking. I know I shouldn't be testing his patience. I know that I'm stuck in a valley surrounded by other vampires, and possibly more demons. I have no way out.

"I know vampires were the first demons. At least, that's what we've come to believe," I begin, swallowing the fear in my throat. My eyes flicker down to the ruby hanging heavy around his neck before I meet his eyes again.

"Is that truly all you know?" he asks quietly, his grip on me loosening a bit. "That we were the first?"

"That, and vampires were created shortly after the Tenth Priestess disappeared. We...we assume the events are related, but we have no proof." I gulp. "*Are* they related?"

"What makes you think I would know?"

"Why else would you care about what knowledge I have? I thought I was just a stupid little human girl?"

Kaius lets me go and turns his back to me, stepping a few paces forward before turning again. "Yes. They're related."

It's silent between us. I stare up at him as he stares back down at me. The tension in his shoulders is on full display as if that's a truth he himself hasn't come to terms with.

And then I begin to wonder how many vampires there are out there who were turned unwillingly. How many people were silly, inconsequential humans like me once, only to be forcefully turned into a monster?

I begin to wonder if Kaius is one of them. In the intimidating crimson of his eyes, there's a sadness there too. Maybe if I oblige him, I can take advantage of that sadness and earn enough sympathy to gain my freedom.

Quietly, I ask, "Will you watch me dance?"

I see shock in his face, in the way the muscles in his jaw fall before returning to their usual stoic expression. He stands up a bit straighter, his shoulders poised more elegantly instead of turned in and tight. His chin is tilted more upward in a regal sort of way. His presence dominates the room, even between just the two of us. The way he holds himself makes me feel...small.

In a world that has always made me feel too big, he's made me feel small. Fragile.

And it's as unsettling as the stillness in the air.

Instead of saying a word, Kaius walks to his chair, heavily sits down, and waits for me with his fingers pressed together in front of his face as if deep in contemplation.

I move to a more open spot in the room, between the end of the bed and the door, and feel the imprint on my wrist.

"How does it work?" I ask quietly.

"You have to let the magic flow through you. Don't try to control it. Be...harmonious with it, and it will bend to your will."

"Bend to my will?" I repeat. "You just told me not to control it."

"Yes, well if it's as stubborn as you, perhaps it won't work at all." He gives me a condescending sneer. "I think

I'd like that better. If it left you in the cold and the dark as I have."

Annoyance races through me and I glare at him before focusing on the mark again. I think first of what I want to dance to. Something light and airy doesn't seem like something he'd enjoy watching. Maybe something darker and melancholy like this palace would be a better fit.

I close my eyes and concentrate—but not too hard—on conjuring a piano. I take a deep breath and imagine it. Black stained wood, pristine white keys, a soft bench to match.

I gasp when a tune plays from behind me and turn around to find a piano has appeared in the corner of my room, and the keys play a haunting tune of their own volition. Like a ghost is performing just for me.

Triumphant, I turn around and cross my arms at Kaius, who's sitting with an amused expression on his face. Dare I say it—he's smiling. That smile disappears as quickly as it came, and I find myself missing it. He's very...human when he smiles. It's comforting and warm in a way he isn't.

I turn my back to ground myself before I begin dancing. My movements are slow, delicate, and technically precise.

Whenever I improvise a dance, I always bring myself to a setting. Tell a story. Play a part. I decide that the tune the piano is playing tells the story of someone who feels isolated and lonely in the world. In a way, I can relate.

My facial expressions turn sorrowful and lamenting. My arms reach for a salvation that isn't there. I imagine I'm in a field of flowers that wilt with each step I take, my pain stealing their life essence. I make them decay as I feel I have.

When I finish my final turn and melt into my end pose, I finally focus on the room around me. Kaius is staring at my feet in what I can only describe as awe. Fascination. Maybe even pride. When I look down to see what he's staring at so intently, my own mouth falls open.

Decaying flowers have sprouted under my feet from the lifeless marble floor.

Kaius stands slowly, sauntering towards me with his icy grace.

"I'm sorry!" I say frantically, seeing the displeasure in his eyes. "I didn't mean to–"

He interrupts me with a gentle touch of the knuckle on his forefinger, tilting my chin up so I have to meet his eyes.

A very small hint of a sly smile touches the corner of his lip.

"It seems you're not as useless as you appear."

With that backhanded attempt at a compliment, I frown and pull my face away from his touch. He raises an eyebrow in challenge, as if to silently ask me if I was truly foolish enough to expect genuine flattery from him. "This was very entertaining. Shall we do it again tomorrow?"

He disappears into the dark hallway with a chuckle, and I purposefully slam the door behind him.

Eight
Kaius

I slouch on my throne in a way that's unbecoming of my station, but with my time with the vampires growing shorter by the minute, I can't find it in me to care about the petty squabbles and politics of my fellow demons. Dravon and I meet often, ensuring that we quickly put an end to any unrest, take count of our livestock, and address any concerns of demon hunter activity in the area.

Instead of listening to Dravon, I sip my blood-laced wine and watch as my pet viper uses my arm as a branch to wind itself around.

This peculiar creature has been with me for over four hundred years. I found him in the Blackwood during a hunt.

Back then, we used to find small caravans of human demon hunters in that wretched place. The plants in the Blackwood and the demons that live there have unique medicinal properties that are incredibly valuable to human apothecaries. Demon hunters make their living by harvesting and collecting these ingredients.

Vampire fangs are incredibly rare and valuable, but for their intoxicating and hallucinogenic affects when crushed into a fine powder and inhaled. One fang could fetch a high enough price for a demon hunter to feed their families for a year, and while I can recognize the irony, we do not enjoy the thought of being hunted for sport and dismantled as trophies.

So, we kill them first. During the hunt where I found Cassius, I traveled with about fifteen vampires. Their orders were to slaughter the hunters, but not before I questioned them, searching decades upon decades for my cursebreaker. When I finally grew tired of always being let down, we simply killed them on sight.

As I was feeding on one of them after our slaughter, I saw this viper coiled up on a rock, watching intently with white eyes. Its scales were black as the void.

Cassius, as I've come to call him, is a puzzling creature. I had suspicions that he was no ordinary viper from the peculiar eye color, but when he long outlived the normal lifespan of a snake, the suspicions were confirmed.

A supernatural being. What, though, I don't know. Perhaps a lost experiment of the Priestesses. It matters not to me. He's been a fine companion. Never one to intrude on my business as a spy would. He comes and goes as he pleases. Sometimes I won't see him for months, only to find him slithering down the corridor or in my study where he likes to sleep between the tomes lining the shelves.

"Lord Kaius," Dravon says, clearing his throat. I glance down from my dais and find him staring at me with bewildered eyes, awaiting intently for my response. "Shall I repeat myself, my Lord?"

Dravon is among the oldest vampires in existence, and for good reason. Even as a human, he was a skilled fighter but even more so, a survivor. He could be stripped naked and pushed into sunlight, and the man would still find a way to slit your throat. He's dangerous, and the entire vampire race knows it, myself included.

But he is no threat to me, and for that I am certain. My demise would only bring about his, and that makes me the most powerful vampire of them all. An immortal king with no subjects brave or stupid enough to challenge my rule.

In another lifetime, in other circumstances, I might even consider Dravon my heir. He is very much my opposite. He's impulsive, short-tempered, melodramatic, and most irritatingly, messy at the dinner table. But what he does or does not do with power and leadership will really be no concern of mine once I'm human.

I wave my hand in a dismissive motion, telling Dravon I'm not at all concerned with what he just said, but still have the decency to let him hear himself talk.

"I asked about the girl." He flips a loose strand of black hair out of his eyes with a quick twitch of his head.

That gives me pause. "The girl?" I reply curtly as I watch Cassius slither around my forearm.

"The human girl that you so clearly wish to keep to yourself. You're not keeping her in with the other cattle?" I give him an unimpressed glare. When I don't respond, Dravon's lip turns into an untrustworthy grin. "*Ah*, not cattle then, but a bed warmer. Do allow me the pleasure of ripping her throat out when you are done with her. She does smell divine."

"You will do no such thing," I warn, though my voice is calm. I want to rouse no suspicions of Adelasia's lingering presence nor her importance to me. She's too valuable for that. Best I let him believe she's just filling my bed. "Are you so concerned about what I do or do not do with my human toys?"

As soon as the words leave my mouth, I feel a tug in the very essence of my being. It catches me off guard and in that insignificant second that I lose focus on my magic, the chandelier hanging from the ceiling falls to the center of the room and shatters the crystals hanging from it.

Cassius slithers away, startled by the loud noise, and Dravon simply steps a foot to the left and kicks away a crystal shard that landed near his boot, unconcerned.

I regain my wits and allow myself a smirk.

I do love it when she's angry.

"You've never taken a human lover," Dravon continues, unfazed by the interruption. "I'm simply...*curious* about what changed."

"The times, Dravon."

With that dismissive tone, Dravon makes his way out of the throne room via the underground passages that allow our kind to wander the valley when the sun is out. When I sense he's gone, I stand to go find the source of the chandelier disturbance.

She's in the center courtyard, watching an insect flutter in a small patch of wildflowers that I suspect she grew herself. They stand out among the dead and decaying foliage that I never cared to tend to.

Unfortunately, the courtyard is one of the few places where the sun is allowed to infiltrate the palace. We vampires use it mostly for admiring the moon and stars. In the daytime, it's lifeless, just like the plants that once grew there.

Adelasia is sitting on the ground with her knees tucked up under her chin. I can smell the anger in her blood, and I can only suspect it stems from the conversation I just had with Dravon.

"Darling, that's what you get for eavesdropping," I say from the safety of the awning that lines the perimeter of the courtyard. Adelasia turns her head and scowls at me.

"Go find another toy to play with," she snaps, and I simply snicker, which only makes her more furious with me. She stands abruptly, conjures a stone in her hand, and throws it.

It lands three feet to the left of me. "Please Adelasia, finish your temper tantrum quickly. Anger spoils your blood, and I do love the way you smell."

"I hate you," she sneers.

"And I hate *you*."

"I haven't even done anything to you!"

"You're violent towards me. You've smacked me, stabbed me, thrown things at me, made a mess of my throne room. You give such an uncivilized response to my hospitality."

Adelasia looks up to the sky and then back to me. She takes a single step backward. "The sun is out. I could run away right now, and you could not chase me."

I use my hand to make a sweeping motion across my body. "Be my guest."

She takes off in a run and I scoff to myself as I watch her disappear down a hill. She's heading East. It's a straight shot from here to the Eastern cave entrance to the valley. She can't miss it.

One of the supernatural abilities vampires possess is speed. I'll use the underground tunnels and cut her off at the cave entrance before she can even make it a mile down the road.

I lean against the cave wall as I wait for her, with my arms and ankles crossed. I can hear her erratic heartbeat and heavy breathing long before she appears in front of me. She nearly falls over as she abruptly stops her sprint when she catches me wave at her from the shadows with a knowing glint in my eyes to reflect her frustrated expression.

Her chest is heaving with effort and she uses a hand to brace herself against the cave wall. Her hair is plastered to her milky skin, covered in a glistening sheen of sweat. Even from across the cave, I can see her pulse in her neck. It's tempting. Intoxicating. I can hear how quickly her blood is running through her veins and I feel my fangs lengthen with the need to lick the salt from her skin before burying them in her neck. Thirst quickly replaces my teasing.

Ever since I tasted that small drop of blood that first night, it's been driving me insane with need. Instincts have me pacing the hallway outside of her bedroom while she sleeps, contemplating another thousand years of immortality just for the divine pleasure of drinking every last drop of her blood.

I know she can see the change in my thoughts.

When vampires are hungry, our eyes turn black, our demeanor becomes dangerous. Every muscle in our body grows taut and ready to pounce. Our vampiric blood rushes to our eyes, our nose, and our ears to heighten our senses for the hunt, making us look even more of a monster than we already are.

Unable to control myself, I have her pinned against the cool cave wall in an instant. Her blood hums with adrenaline and fear and my fangs grow even longer, desperate to drink deeply from that pounding vein in her neck.

My mouth falls open with a thousand words I want to say, but the thirst keeps them trapped in my throat. "I...I need to taste," I whisper. I close my eyes and growl as my fingers dig into the stone of the cave wall, crushing it under the ruthlessness of my grip. "Adelasia, run into the sunlight." When she doesn't move, I punch the wall, causing the entire cave to rumble. "Now!"

I can only stop myself for a second before I chase her out of the cave. She falls to the black stone ground lit by the bright sun just as I reach the entrance. My body trembles as I glare at her neck; I'm still wild with thirst at the sight of her. I can't think about anything else.

I need it. I need her.

Though she's in the sunlight, I find myself less aware of the pain of the sun and grab her ankle and pull her to me, grunting through my teeth as the light burns the skin of my hand. Adelasia whimpers as I drag her beneath me, pinning her legs down with my weight. I use one arm to tug her head to the side by her hair and the other to pin her remaining hand above her head. Adelasia struggles underneath me as hard as she can, but it's no use. I'm too strong. Too thirsty. Too uncontrollable.

"Kaius, please," Adelasia begs. "Please don't."

"I need to," I growl against her throat.

"Don't hurt me."

"It won't hurt. You'll feel nothing...but pure...*euphoria.*"

My fangs touch the delicate skin of her neck. I can practically taste her sweet blood already.

"Lord Kaius," a voice grumbles from behind me just as her skin is about to give way to my bite. I glance over my shoulder to see Dravon grinning. The shadows fall over his sharp features and dark hair, making him appear more dangerous. "You know it's rude to feed in public and not offer to share."

The sense returns to me at his voice.

He wants Adelasia. He wants what's mine. *He wants to taste her blood as I have.*

I suddenly become territorial in a way that's almost foreign to me. I pull her and I to our feet, turn around, and shove the girl behind me so that Dravon cannot see her. I hold her there by her wrist so she cannot run.

"Perhaps I wasn't clear in the throne room, but she is not for sharing. She is *mine*. Find a female from my collection of cattle if it pleases you. Take ten of them if you must, but you will *not* have her. This is the last we will speak of it."

Dravon's head tilts up in acceptance though his face shows he's insulted by the obvious dismissal. He's never liked being told no. "Very well," he concedes, and then he peeks around my body to look at Adelasia. "Perhaps I'll enjoy my feast in the room next to hers, so she can hear them scream."

"Leave her be," I warn.

Dravon snickers. "You do love it when they scream, don't you, my Lord?"

I don't answer. Dravon scoffs and then enters a set of tunnels that connects the opposite side of the valley to this cave, directly across from the one I came through. I face Adelasia once again and with a forceful but not painful grip on her toned bicep, I lead her back to the palace through the tunnels.

When we reach her suite, I let her go roughly. She stumbles into the room and clumsily tries to shut me out with the door. I stop her efforts with my foot.

She gasps and looks up at me. I can see the fear still in her eyes. There's a red scratch on her neck from where my fangs dug into the skin, though not deep enough to draw blood.

"Be careful the next time you run. There are worse monsters than me lurking in the shadows," I warn.

I move my foot, and she shuts the door in my face. I can hear her collapse to her knees just inside. Her erratic heartbeat and uneven breathing tell me she's in a panic.

I'd offer her no comfort, so I leave her alone with her distress.

I need to feed before I break down her door. I was feral in that cave. I haven't been so blind with bloodlust in centuries. I was in such a craze I was truly considering ruining my first and possibly *only* chance at a mortal life.

I'm not a man who worries about many things, but that is concerning on a level I can't even begin to describe.

I run into one of the human servants in the hallway outside my bed chamber, carrying an armful of fresh linens. A male. Tall. Strong. His blood will be good.

I shove him against the nearest wall. For the first time in centuries, I completely lose myself in the bloodlust and feed until I feel him go limp and lifeless in my arms.

But I don't stop there. I feed and feed and feed until the palace is littered with bloodless human bodies.

Dravon finds me at the end of my bloodletting, hunched in a corner attempting to regain control of my own body, nearly in tears at how badly I want to stop but can't.

Dravon has witnessed this many times in our years as vampires, but he is not one for sympathy. In fact, I think he finds it borderline pathetic how hard I fight against my supernatural instincts.

However, when he finds me in my craze, he simply approaches me in silence and hands me a cloth from his jacket to wipe my face.

I take it, and then I hear him snicker, but it doesn't quite sound like him. There's something too eerie about his voice. Something off. I look at him with suspicion, but he continues to give me a knowing grin.

"Why fight it, my Lord?"

My hand is still shaking with the bloodlust, but I meet my friend's eyes and give him a stern warning with nothing but my expression, before shoving his handkerchief into his chest and entering my bedchamber.

I conjure myself a bath, and while I sit in the hot water and remember the ghostly feeling of warm blood in my veins, I listen for Adelasia's heartbeat.

I tap the edge of the marble tub to the same rhythm with my index finger.

Tap tap. Tap tap. Tap tap.

Nine
Adelasia

I have not seen Kaius in five days. Not since he nearly fed on me in the cave and one of his vampire advisors stopped him. I can't tell if he's staying away from me because he's still ready to sink his teeth into me, or because a part of him feels bad for what he did. I fear it's the former.

For humans, it's a horrific violation to be fed on involuntarily. It's why we consider vampires such savages and why we fear them so wholly—women especially. The more uncivilized vampires in the world will raid cities and towns, feeding on the women while violating their bodies. We're nothing but vessels for food and pleasure for them.

I've never understood why some humans choose that life. They offer themselves to the vampires, and they get nothing in return. Kaius told me they're called cattle, and it's just another sickening way they dehumanize us.

Though I haven't seen Kaius in days, I have explored the palace a bit more. I found an empty, unused room of mirrors on the second floor covered in cobwebs, and with the limited magic Kaius gifted me, I was able to turn it into a dance studio, and that's where I spend most of my time if not in my room for sleep or meals.

No one ever bothers me here—not even the servants. It's just me, and the enchanted instruments I conjured to play music for me while I dance.

They've become somewhat friends, in a very sad, lonely sort of way. They seem to be in tune with my emotions and always play the perfect accompanying music to my moods. Lately, I've been nothing but melancholy. I miss the sun. I miss my bed. I miss my friends at the company.

Most of all, I miss my mother.

My heart aches every time I think about her, worried sick about me. She has no idea if I'm alive or dead. The last memory she'll have of me is the way I screamed when I was kidnapped right in front of her eyes. I imagine that's a parent's worst nightmare—to have your only living child go missing without a trace.

The instruments stop their tune and tears prick in my eyes as I land a leap in the silence of the room. My shoes echo loudly off the cold floors, and I pinch the bridge of my nose to keep myself from sobbing. I hear the door open behind me, and I huff in frustration, expecting it to be Kaius.

I turn to find a small woman standing in the doorway with a silver tray in her hand, and a ceramic bowl no bigger than my palm in the center. Steam rises from the bowl, and the woman's face grows rosy from the heat. *A human!*

"Miss Adelasia," she says uncomfortably under my stare. "Lord Kaius asked me to bring this to you." She gestures down to the bowl. "I promise it's not as bad as it smells."

I take a few steps towards her. She's a tiny thing. Standing at least a foot shorter than me. She's young, barely twenty if I had to guess. Her hazel eyes are warm and friendly, perfectly accompanying her golden blonde hair.

I look at the steaming bowl. "What is it?"

"Just some herbs and spices, nothing dangerous. It smells horrid but you don't need to drink it but once a month."

I give her a strange look, and she realizes she didn't answer my question. "Oh..." she chuckles awkwardly. "It's for the women. So we don't...bleed."

My nose turns upwards in disgust. "You mean so we don't get pregnant when these immortal men take what isn't theirs."

The thought of Kaius sending this to me so he can prepare me for mounting causes bile to snake its way up my throat. I want to find him right now and drive a stake through his heart. How immortality destroys any sense of right and wrong disgusts me to the point it makes me dizzy.

"No!" the woman gasps as if I've said something inappropriate. "Our monthly cycles...they can smell it. It drives the vampires mad, and this keeps them docile. Vampires can't breed with humans."

I blink in confusion. "They can't?"

The woman shakes her head and gestures towards the cup. She's right, it does smell horrid, but I take it from her and swallow the contents in three big gulps. I purse my lips as the unpleasant mixture runs down my throat.

"Male vampires are infertile," she explains. My cheeks turn pink on their own accord for thinking so lowly of Kaius. In all fairness, he's never caused any harm to me that I didn't ask for by provoking him. The young woman smiles and curtseys to me. "I'm Iphigenia. I'm to be your personal servant."

"You're a human," I point out. "Did they kidnap you?"

She seems perturbed by the assumption. "No! Lord Kaius *saved* me. My village was attacked by a pack of werebeasts. My three younger sisters and I were the only survivors. His men fought off the beasts and found us hiding under some rubble, injured and frightened. His men wanted to feed on us. We had no family and no home, and we were just young girls. I thought we were going to die that day, but Lord Kaius claimed us—no *not* that way—just...he told us he'd spare us and provide food and shelter if we helped take care of the other humans living here. That was four years ago. I was fifteen then. My sisters were all younger than ten. I knew I couldn't provide for them myself, so I accepted his offer, and we've been here ever since."

Poor thing. What a horrible experience, to lose your family to werebeasts and live under the nose of even worse demons. Though, in a way, that's what's happened to me.

"What about you?" she asks, and by the way she looks around the room, I can see the tiniest hint of jealousy in her eyes at my freedom. Kaius has never asked me to earn my keep. In fact, I've intentionally defied every rule he's made for me.

"I'm a prisoner," I answer.

"You don't look like a prisoner to me. Prisoners tend to wear chains, not ribbons and silk."

"He kidnapped me. Two of his vampire servants stole me right in front of my entire town. In front of my mother."

She narrows her eyes at me, and then her face softens. "You're to be his bride then?"

I laugh with genuine amusement. *What a preposterous thought.* "I'd rather stake my own heart than live the rest of my life tied to that man."

As I finish filling her ears with that venom, from the corner of my eye, I see a fast movement near my feet. I look down and let out a squeal as I jump slightly to the side. A large, black snake watches me as I back towards the wall. I breathe heavy in concern, but the viper comes no closer to me.

Iphigenia lets out a quiet laugh. "Don't worry about Cassius. He's the Blood King's companion. He's friendly," she leans over slightly to whisper to me, "But watch your bed. He likes to curl up under the warm covers."

She says it with such a fondness for the creature that I trust her sincerity and let my guard down.

"*Kaius* and *Cassius*," I hum sarcastically. "How creative."

Iphigenia smiles at me and then squats down to gently pat Cassius' head. "I've been here for much longer than you have, Miss, and I can tell you with certainty that Lord Kaius doesn't do anything without a clear reason. Try not to judge him too harshly."

I scoff. "Judge him?! What *noble* reason would he have for kidnapping a dancer? Hm? Is he lacking in entertainment here in this depressing palace?"

"I can't answer that for him," Iphigenia says, and then she and Cassius leave me to my solitude in the room of mirrors.

I dance for several more hours, until my skin is damp with a thin layer of sweat, my muscles ache from overuse, and my stomach cries painfully for food.

I leave the studio and wander through the halls. Empty and barren just like every other room here. These immortals have lived dozens of lifetimes, and it unsettles me that their homes are so lifeless in comparison. They could have beautiful, ancient, ornate architecture, but instead opt for plain walls, plain ceilings, and plain floors.

The outside of this palace is stunning, but the inside is nothing more than a well-polished box.

I hear a commotion and some instinct within me tells me to hide, so I crouch behind a brazier and peek around it.

Down the corridor, I see the vampire that stopped Kaius from feeding on me in the cave, with a leash in one hand and a whip in the other. If I remember rightly from my eavesdropping, his name is Dravon.

At the other end of the leash is the man from the prison. The sickly one. He's wearing only trousers, his bones sticking out to a disturbing degree. There are scars covering his back from a whip—some new, some old. He's covered in dirt and blood.

The vampire whips the man while he scrubs the floor clean of dirt that isn't there and his own blood. Dravon has a vile grin on his face as he tortures that poor man. What could he have possibly done to deserve this?

I can't just hide and watch. I have to do something. Do I dare stand up to Dravon without Kaius here to protect me?

Before I can talk myself out of it, I stand up and walk towards them.

"Leave him alone!" I demand. Dravon looks at me and then down to the man. With a grin, Dravon spits and kicks him before dropping the leash and walking towards me. We stand at the same height, yet his coldness easily overshadows me. My cheeks heat as my false bravery crumbles. Dravon gently hooks his finger into the high neckline of my leotard, examining the skin underneath.

"Curious," he says quietly. With another grin, he steps around me and disappears down the hall.

I rush to the man curled in the fetal position on the ground and kneel next to him. He whimpers when I touch his temple, where a soft stream of blood drips into his eyes.

"Here," I say quietly, using the magic Kaius gave me to conjure him a goblet of water. His parched, chapped lips tremble as he takes a careful sip before drinking the rest. I refill the goblet again. "Drink as much as you need," I tell him. He eyes me suspiciously over the rim of the cup.

"You're a human," he croaks, his voice hoarse and strained.

I nod. I shimmy out of the skirt I have on over my leotard and use it to soak up some of the blood on his face as he drinks. "What's your name?"

"Saddiq."

"Where are you from, Saddiq?"

"The Cambouri Desert. The westernmost part of the al-Abadi region."

"My father visited the Desert once, before I was born. He told me that the sand is the most beautiful shade of orange, and there are strange spiky plants in the ground that hold water so crisp it could quench any thirst." Saddiq gives me a half-hearted smile, and behind his eyes I can see the way he misses his home. "I'm Adelasia."

"Why did you help me?" he asks. "He could have killed you."

"He won't," I answer, even though I'm unsure of how true that is. "The Vampire Lord has forbidden him from touching me." Saddiq eyes me suspiciously at that but continues to drink. My eyes trace along his skin and bones for legs. He's so frail. I attempt to conjure some food for him, but I've not yet mastered this strange magic Kaius gave me, and my attempts are, quite literally, fruitless.

"I'm going to bring you some food. Stay here. Drink," I instruct, before standing and rushing towards the kitchen. My nose carries me to the smell of roasting meat and sauteed vegetables. When I step into the kitchen, the vampires and human servants alike pay no attention to me. They walk past me as if I'm invisible.

Laid out on the long center table of the kitchen are trays of cheeses, fruits, and nuts. I pop a grape into my mouth and take a few handfuls of food.

As I reach for a thick slice of warm bread, a cold hand snatches my wrist, causing me to drop the cheese and fruit I had in my fist. I gasp and look up to find a particularly vile-looking vampire staring at me with distaste. His face is sallow, just like the vampires that kidnapped me.

"What do we have here?" he asks rhetorically. Some of the servants look over their shoulders at us, but most still pay no mind. "Looks like one of the cows has wandered out of the pen."

I try to tug my wrist free. "Let me go," I demand forcefully.

"You know cattle aren't allowed in the kitchens."

"It's a good thing I'm not cattle then. Let me go!" I shout. The vampire only snickers and drags me across the kitchen until my back is flat against the wall. He holds me by my neck so forcefully I can only take shallow, unsatisfying breaths.

"Kai...Kaius said..."

"'*Kaius said*'? Did you hear that?" he shouts over his shoulder, drawing the attention of the rest of the kitchen staff. "Disobedient *and* disrespectful. Lord Kaius won't miss you, I think. He'll like you better mixed in with his wine."

My head feels like it's going to pop from the pressure of being choked, and the vampire laughs. "Or maybe I'll just have you for dinner myself."

His fangs grow longer and he releases my throat only to tug my head to the side and give himself access to my neck.

The vampire lunges for me, and I scream as I brace myself and close my eyes for the pain, but it doesn't come. The room goes silent. No more clattering of pans. Even the roasting fire seems to go quiet.

I peek to find Kaius clutching the vampire that's holding onto me by the neck. His face is the picture of indifference. His body is loose, the only sign of tension at all is the bruising grip his fingers have on the other vampire.

The rest of the servants have all knelt to the floor, their eyes locked on Kaius as if awaiting instruction—or punishment.

A muscle in Kaius' jaw flexes and he tilts his head back to examine the man he has in his grasp with disgust. "What seems to be the problem here?"

The vampire shakily points to me. "The cattle—"

Kaius squeezes his throat tighter. "I seem to recall hearing her tell you that she is not cattle all the way from the other side of the palace. Are you calling my guest a liar, worm?"

"No...no of course not."

Kaius gives him a humorless smile and lets him go. "Good."

"My sincere apologies, my Lord. I meant no offense to you."

"No, of course not. You'd be foolish to purposely offend me," Kaius agrees before turning to me. "What about you, Adelasia? Did this *worm—*" he glares at the vampire who seems to shrink at the degrading tone in Kaius' voice, "offend you?"

It goes silent again, and I realize he's waiting for my response. I open my mouth, but no words come out, so I simply shake my head. Kaius nods, and his eyes catch on the handful of fruit and cheese I dropped that sits discarded on the ground.

He uses a hand to motion towards the table in the center of the room. "Please help yourself."

I approach the table. My hands tremble as I pick out another selection of fruits, nuts and cheese.

I hear an awful squelch behind me.

I've heard that sound before, when Kaius ripped out the heart of the two vampires that kidnapped me.

Just as I was that night, I'm stupid enough to turn my head and look. Kaius steps over the dead body and one of the servants hands him a wet cloth to clean his hands. The dead vampire turns to ash, and the servants return to their duties.

I make every attempt to avoid eye contact as I gather the food again, leave the kitchen, and make my way back through the halls to Saddiq.

When I get to where I left him, he's nowhere to be found, and the water goblet I gave him sits discarded on its side.

"Looking for something?"

I huff at the voice behind me before turning to face Dravon. I give him my best scowl, and he gives me an insincere grin in return.

"Where is he?"

"What concern is it to you?"

"*Where is he?*" I repeat.

From down the hall, I catch Kaius in my peripheral vision, and as quickly as we make eye contact from afar, he's at my side, examining Dravon suspiciously. Then, he looks at me. "What is it?" he asks me.

"The prisoner, Saddiq. I want to know where he is," I tell him without breaking my hateful stare at Dravon.

Kaius looks to his advisor. "Tell her," he commands. Dravon narrows his eyes at me. "Now."

Dravon's jaw moves from side to side in annoyance. "Dungeon," he replies. He barely moves his shoulder to avoid bumping into me when he walks around us. I huff and look at Kaius, who is obviously awaiting an explanation.

"He was hurting him. Whipping him and then forcing him to clean up his own blood."

"Dravon has always been a sadist," Kaius says, then he looks at the food in my arms. "You weren't in the kitchen for yourself."

"No, I wasn't," I confirm. "Please take me to him."

Kaius nods towards the long end of the hallway as a gesture to follow him. He leads me down several flights of stairs and out of the palace, taking me directly to the dungeon in the cool moonlight. When we arrive, I rush straight to Saddiq's cell and kneel. He looks surprised.

"You came," he says, and then he gulps sadly at the food, as if he believes this is a trick and that it will turn to ash in his mouth.

I nod as I push the food through the space between the cell bars. Saddiq grabs the food as if it's the last thing he'll ever eat, his body so malnourished that he gags on it as it slivers down his throat. I look at Kaius. "Can't you let him out?"

Kaius examines the bars and wraps his cold fingers around them. He pulls, but unlike the cell I was in when I first met him, the door does not give. He tries again. Still nothing.

"It's enchanted," he says. "I do not know this ward. I will have to go through Dravon to break it."

I scowl. Not necessarily at Kaius, but at the thought of Dravon forcing us to leave Saddiq here. I sigh and gently reach a hand through the bars to touch Saddiq's bony shoulder.

"I'll come back every day with food or clothes or whatever you need. I promise."

He gives my hand an untrusting glare, alternating between it and Kaius. "Why?"

I give him a soft smile. "The one thing these demons will never take from me is my humanity."

Ten

Kaius

I lead Adelasia back to her suite in silence, and the entire time I can feel her thoughts. Perhaps it's because it's been so long since I've had cause to truly care about another, but it intrigues me how invested she's become in the wellbeing of Dravon's prisoner.

What concerns me though, is that I can tell that she's angry with me for allowing it.

As if she needed another reason to believe I'm a monster.

Her last words about not losing her humanity have been repeating in my head over and over since they fell from her lips.

Behind the closed door of her bedroom, she turns to me, nearly knocking me over with the intensity of her stare.

"Make him set Saddiq free," she demands.

I nod slightly. "I shall speak with him," I tell her truthfully. The magic on the cell door is unknown to me, and I've never known Dravon to care much for the arcane.

So where did he learn it from? Even with Yekaterina's Bloodstone hanging from my neck, I was unable to break through his ward. I find that deeply disturbing and I intend to find out who Dravon has been speaking with to learn and execute such magic.

"That's it?" she asks. "You'll '*speak*' with him? What if he refuses?"

"Adelasia, I understand that you don't wish to see a human suffer as he has, but I have known Dravon for many lifetimes and he is not someone that you can get through by politely asking," I sigh and straighten my shoulders slightly. "I will handle it."

That seems to satisfy her for the time being. She takes a deep breath and turns to the mirror on her vanity. She takes out the pins in her hair one by one until her long black locks fall freely down her back. The light from the fireplace reflects from it, creating a deep amber color that makes her eyes stand out even more than they normally do.

She breaks me out of my thoughts when she clears her throat, noticing that I'm staring at her.

I clear my own throat. "I apologize. You...your eyes..."

"My eyes?" she whispers, leaning closer to the mirror searching for some flaw that isn't there. "What's wrong with my eyes?"

"Absolutely nothing," I answer. That's all I offer.

She looks down slightly. "Thank you for earlier...in the kitchen. How did you know I was there?"

I take a few steps closer to her until I'm directly at her back, yet she cannot see me in the mirror as I see her. She stares into the void where my body should be, her mind trying to understand what it cannot see. I take my hand and gently move some of her hair out of the way so I can reach around her to place my hand on her heart.

"It may not seem so, but the human heart is loud. Yours beats like drums in my ears. I can hear you, always. I simply followed the echoes when you began to panic."

"You killed him," she whispers.

"Yes," I confirm.

"Because I was scared?"

"Because he threatened you."

She takes a deep breath, still staring through my non-existent reflection.

"Tell me why I'm really here." She turns to face me, stepping to the side slightly so she isn't trapped between the vanity and me. "Because I know you think I'm just a useless, stupid human–but you don't make me work like Iphigenia, you keep me hidden from most other vampires, and you...resist the clear urge you have to feed on me."

The corner of my mouth turns up into a smile. "Do you want me to feed on you, Adelasia?" I take a step towards her, so she takes one back. "Are you offended that I indulge in others and not you?" Another step towards her. Another step back. And another and another until I'm caging her against the cold wall and my long arms. "My hesitation does not stem from a lack of desire. I thought that would have been made clear in the caves when you ran from me." I smile wide enough to show her my elongating fangs. "There are few things I want more in this immortal life than to drink from you. To feel you writhe less and less until you give into the pleasure it brings before turning into an animal, as hungry with it as I am."

She takes a shaky breath. "Is that what happens?"

"Humans always wish to know the truth despite the false sense of security it gives. It's often the thing you'll end up fearing the most," I respond. I lean down to be closer to her ear. "Why do you think humans come to offer themselves? Because it brings them pleasure beyond anything they can experience in their world." I blow softly on the sensitive curve of her neck. I can hear and feel her heart begin to race faster. I smirk against her neck before very softly touching my tongue to her skin. I pull back and our eyes meet. I cup her warm cheek with my large, cold hand and gently rub my thumb along her bottom lip.

She gulps, and I smell the fear spike in her blood. I know she can tell I've noticed in the way the blood vessels under my eyes begin to grow darker and they turn from red to black. I grip her chin and tilt her head to the side, watching the vein pulsate in her throat.

"Why not just kill me now?" she shakily asks.

"Waste not, sweet Adelasia," I whisper, before leaning in once more and lightly nipping at her pulse point. She whimpers, and instantly, my fangs ache. Her delicate flesh would give way so easily. I'm standing somewhere on the precipice of insanity and self-control.

I could do it, I think to myself. *Just a taste. Just one. Enough to savor it.* The beautiful irony of my most desired taste of human blood and my recovered mortality stemming from her sweet veins.

Agony.

Irony.

Poetry.

At the cost of what? A little prick to her neck? A fleeting moment of pain before it turns into pleasure for us both?

She already thinks I'm a monster. Why not solidify that belief and quench my thirst for her in one fell swoop?

I can feel her feeble attempts to push me back—the soft pounding of her small fists on my chest. As she uses all her strength to fight me off, I gently hold her head to the side and watch the vein in her neck. I can practically hear the blood rushing through her veins now.

I need it. I cannot hold back anymore.

I need *her*.

I feel her fingers claw at my chest, and when her palm accidentally touches the ruby around my neck, she tightens her fingers around it unconsciously.

It's the dark magic taking hold of her, and I know it's reached her soul when I hear her scream. It's not a scream from this world, though. Her screams echo through every plane of existence. Through the heavens and the hells and perhaps even the other lifetimes we might have lived.

The agony in her wails is something I relate to deep in the core of my being. I felt such a way once, too. The terror, the confusion, the anger. It breaks me out of my bloodlust almost instantly.

The Bloodstone is clenched so tight in her fist that I'm worried I might break her fingers trying to pry it away from her. I have to help somehow. The dark magic that emanates from these gems is far too horrific for the mortal mind. She crumbles to the ground as she thrashes and screams in my arms. Tears from beyond her consciousness pour out of her eyes.

I have no idea what Yekaterina could be showing her or saying to her through her twisted magic, but Adelasia does not deserve to witness that wickedness. I shush and coo at her as I carefully pry the gem from her hands. Her thin fingers are so delicate, and each one trembles as I loosen her fist.

When I manage to free her from the gem's influence, she stops her screaming, but she's no less traumatized from the experience. She cries and cries in my arms as I rock her gently in a soft embrace. I have no idea how to comfort others. I've never had to. I'm certain she can feel my hesitation and how uncomfortable this affection is making me in the stiffness of my body.

I stroke her hair in silence until her breathing grows even again. When she finally finds the courage to meet my gaze, she reaches up a hand and cups my cheek. The action is so tender, so foreign, that I flinch. Her warm fingertips graze my cheek, and her lip begins to quiver again.

"I saw you," she whispers, the horror still lingering in her shaky voice. "Blood was running down the corners of your mouth and down your neck. You were crying as you held a woman to your chest."

I have no strength to continue to look at her. Not when she talks about that memory. It was the most painful day of my entire existence.

"Kaius...who was that woman?"

I close my eyes and turn my head further away from her. She uses her soft hand on my cheek to make me look at her. I grind my teeth and beg her with my eyes to stop asking.

"What else did you see?" I ask, attempting to steer her thoughts away from the worst day of my life. She pulls out of my arms slightly and wipes the remaining wetness from her cheeks away. I lean against the foot of her bed, and she sits with her knees tucked to her chest, facing me.

"It was awful," she finally says. "It felt like I was trapped underwater. It was so dark. I couldn't breathe. All around me, demons and monsters circled and lunged for me. There was...a woman dressed in tattered robes and a broken headdress. In between the rips of the fabric, I saw rotting flesh. Maggots falling from her eyes. She reached out and pulled me away from the monsters. She pulled me close and wept as she stuck a silver dagger through my chest. I fell to the ground, but the ground wasn't there. I was falling and falling into a void with no end until I finally landed and saw you. I...I tried to call for you. I asked for your help, but you couldn't hear me. You were holding that woman and crying."

Something compels me to take her hand in mine. She lets me line up our palms. "Are you okay?"

She nods. "I think so."

We both observe where our hands are touching, and then she asks, "What are these markings?"

My hand, wrist, and forearm are covered in black swirls, extending from my forefinger to my elbow. The intricate patterns take me back to a time in my life centuries ago that I've spent so long wishing I could forget.

I sigh. "They're the sign of...a broken promise."

She huffs in frustration. "You're not good at giving straight answers."

"Well if I told you all my secrets, they wouldn't very much be secrets anymore would they?" I tease before my face falls. "I have a lot of them, Adelasia. A millennium's worth."

"Keeping your pain bottled up inside isn't the same as having secrets. It just means you're suffering alone."

She's right. Of course, she is. She's more observant and empathetic than she has any right to be. I expected her to be half-witted and frightened, but she stood up for herself and others and asked questions where anyone else would have cowered. She even stood up to Dravon and lived to tell the tale. That alone is an extraordinary feat.

I envy her; to be so needed without even knowing why. A feeling of guilt settles heavy in my chest and I hate it. I've waited over a thousand years to find her, guilt should be nowhere on the list of emotions I have.

"Was she a lover?" Adelasia asks.

My sorrowful thoughts pause as my brow furrows. "What?"

"The woman you were holding...was she a lover?"

I sigh and place my hand at my side. "No. But I did love her."

"I'm very sorry. I've known the pain of losing someone you love, too. And I know it never gets any easier."

"Did you lose a lover?"

"No. My father and brother. My brother was a free spirit. Where I enjoyed the vanity and attention of being on the stage, he was more in touch with his wild side. He always wanted to be outdoors. He would wade through the forests barefoot, and come back covered in dirt. My mom would always get so upset when he would trek mud into the house. He had an eye for fruits and mushrooms and could always tell which ones were safe to eat and which were poisonous. He was only two years younger than me and made a decent living foraging for the merchants in the marketplace. My father would go out into the forests with him and hunt wild game. They were chased and mauled by werebeasts, left to die in the streets of my town. My father was already dead, but I was holding my brother when he died. I've never forgotten the way it broke me to feel him exhale only to never inhale again."

"Werebeasts, not vampires?" I ask. "Then why do you hate vampires so much?"

"I hate *all* demons. They were created only to bring humans misery, and that's certainly all they've ever caused me."

My shoulders sag, and for the first time in a long time, I feel vulnerable. "I feel the same, you know."

To my shock, she reaches forward to place her hand over mine. "You never wanted to be a vampire."

She's so smart. It doesn't surprise me that she came to that conclusion so quickly. I tilt my chin down slightly. "I was cursed."

My eyes close and I find myself soaking in the feeling of her warm skin touching mine so softly. Her thumb lightly brushes across my knuckles. I haven't felt something so tender from a human in a long time, and never would have expected it from her.

"It was my mother," I say quietly.

Her thumb stops stroking along my hand. I feel the new rigidity in her body. I feel her slipping away again, ready to damn me and call me a monster.

"She was my first victim. I was newly changed and had no understanding of what I had become. I felt…sick. Shaky and feverish. Hungry yet nauseous. This was long before modern medicine had become common practice…when a fever easily meant death. I went to my mother for help because I was terrified. She took one look at me and knew something was wrong. I fell into her arms and my head landed in the crook of her neck…and I felt her blood pulsing through her skin. I could smell it. I could taste it in the air. I didn't even know what I was doing when I sunk my teeth into her neck."

I feel an uncomfortable burning sensation behind my eyes and a pain in my chest, built on guilt and anger and regret.

"She was dead and cold in my arms before I even came to my senses and realized what I had done. If killing her wasn't bad enough...the state I left her body in was horrific. Her throat was ripped open. Her nails were broken and bloody from trying to claw at me to get me to stop. She had bald spots in her hair from when I grabbed it so tight to keep her head still that I ripped it clean out of her scalp. Her lifeless eyes were filled with shock and betrayal."

I feel something wet fall down my cheek. Tears.

Disgusting.

I frown at myself and wipe them away. "I held her and wept for three days before the Tenth Priestess found me. And do you know what she did, Adelasia?" My face twists at the memory. "She plucked out my mother's right eye and staked it through the sharp crown atop her head."

"Kaius..."

"I killed her," I admit quietly. "I ripped that crown from her head and shoved it into her throat before pulling out her spine. And when the other Priestesses found out about what I had done to their beloved sister, they cursed me again, and said that the only way I could earn my mortality back is if I released their sister's soul back to this plane of existence."

"How do you release her soul?"

"A ritual."

Adelasia scoffs and rolls her eyes. "And here I thought we were bonding. We're back to vague answers I see."

That pulls my mouth into a small, but fake smile. "Secrets, Adelasia."

She moves to sit with her back against the bed as I am, the length of our long legs touching. She's the tallest woman I've ever seen, aside from the Priestesses. All ten of them could touch the sky with their fingertips, made of beautiful long lines and expressive hands. They wore long veils in shades of black and gray that covered them head to toe. It was considered a great honor to see their faces. I saw them once. Yekaterina introduced me at the height of our passionate love affair. I thought they would make me powerful. Desirable. Rich.

But instead, I let them steal everything I held dear, and then they punished me for retaliating.

Adelasia is so unlike them despite sharing their physical features. Tall stature. Sharp cheekbones. Long hair. Their skin colors varied depending on which part of the world they came from, but they always shared this otherworldly beauty that women and men alike can only dream of possessing.

Despite what legends say, they're not all inherently evil. They can be spiteful and wicked, yes, and they punished me harshly for killing their sister, but many of them simply want to see that all creatures, demons and humans alike, live in harmony with nature. Perhaps not with each other, but with the earth. They all have unprecedented affinities for magic, and four of them fancy the Four Elements, Air, Water, Earth, and Fire. Gaia, the Earth Priestess, is quite pleasant, and the only one who seemed distraught by what Yekaterina had done to me.

But her loyalty to her sisters outweighed her conscience, and she cursed me anyway.

In an attempt to change the subject, I look at Adelasia's feet in her dancing shoes. "Adelasia, tell me why you dance."

Her feet flex into perfect arches and she sighs as if she's been waiting her entire life for someone to ask that exact thing.

"Because if you go anywhere in the world...any culture, any time of day or night, amid war or famine and all other sufferings, dancing brings joy. It's a language all its own, that can be spoken to anyone, anywhere, and you'll always find someone willing to share in that joy with you."

I huff, because I was expecting her to say that she enjoyed the attention. I have a bad habit of assuming the worst in her, but then again, she does the same for me.

"I'd like to feel joy again."

Adelasia places her hand gently on my thigh. "What's stopping you?"

"My joy comes at a cost I'm not sure I'm willing to pay anymore."

"What does that mean?"

I take her hand in my own and lift it to my lips to kiss her knuckles. "Goodnight, Adelasia," I whisper, and then stand up to leave without another word.

Eleven
Adelasia

Three days pass, and the palace seems more lively than usual. The normally silent halls are now teeming with whispers and chatter from humans and vampires alike, who all seem...cheerful.

When I step into my dance studio, even the enchanted instruments seem to shoot up in excitement at the sight of me.

"I don't suppose you can tell me why everyone seems to have such high spirits today?" I ask absently to the violin, which only swivels from left to right in response.

I take a place on the floor and begin to stretch my muscles. The violin begins to play something soft in the background. I close my eyes and let the music fill my heart, and once my body feels ready, I begin to secure the ribbons of my shoes around my ankles. Unfortunately, when I go to test their stability, I'm disappointed to find the arch of the shoe completely limp. Dead. They're too worn and I don't want to risk injury.

I take them off and feel a bit emotional as I drop them in the corner of the room. They were the only pair I had. One small relic I was able to bring with me to this new life.

I hear the door open behind me and glance up to see Kaius standing there. "Do you mind if I watch you today?" he asks, motioning to an empty wingback chair in the corner of the room that has suddenly appeared.

"Only if you tell me why the entirety of the palace isn't so depressing for once." He nods and takes a seat in his chair. "A straight answer this time," I clarify. He tilts his chin down and rests his ankle on his knee. I spy the hilt of a silver dagger in his boot. There's a large ruby embedded in the pommel, perfectly matching the shade of the one around his neck.

I never noticed it before, but ever since I touched the ruby and became flooded with his dreadful memories, I've come to realize that the gemstone around his neck hums with a dark aura. It's faint, but I can see and feel it…almost reaching for me, and I find myself wanting to reach back.

"Adelasia," Kaius whispers, and his hand softly rests on my hip as he looks up at me from the chair. I hadn't realized that I'd been approaching him slowly, stuck in a trance. "It's not your fault. It preys on uncorrupted people like you." His thumb gently brushes over my hip bone. "I won't let it hurt you."

"It's dangerous then?"

"No."

I chuckle uncomfortably as I back away with my hands pointedly behind my back. "I'm not sure I believe you."

"It's not dangerous because I will protect you."

"Why would you protect me? What am I to you?"

"So many questions."

"So little answers."

"Dance, Adelasia," he warns, though teasingly. He glances down to my feet. "Where are your shoes?"

"Dead," I say. He raises an eyebrow. "Oh? You wish for further explanation I see."

He grins. "You're lucky I enjoy your company. That smart mouth of yours is nothing but trouble."

I slightly roll my eyes. "When shoes are dead, it means they're worn out. It causes unnecessary strain on my feet and ankles. I can go through a pair of shoes in just one day if it's a particularly brutal class. Mine were already on their last leg when I was...taken."

Something in his face falls then, as if he doesn't like to remind himself that he's taken me from my human life.

I shrug my shoulders. "It doesn't matter," I whisper, then take a spot in the center of the room and look over my shoulder towards the instruments in the opposite corner from Kaius. "Something cheerful then? To irritate your good master while he broods over there in the corner."

The instruments seem to perk up and a moment later, the strings begin to play a quick, lovely tune that makes me feel as though I'm racing through a vibrant forest lit by the gentle luminescence of fireflies.

It's been a long time since I've danced like this without my pointe shoes, but after a small adjustment period, I feel...uninhibited. The technical constraints of ballet no longer govern my movements, and I let the music take me to a world filled with light, joy, and laughter. Filled with freedom. Filled with dazzling turns and high leaps and dynamic lines.

The instruments know when my body begins to grow tired and the tune begins to soften and slow. Afterward, when my chest is heaving and my brow is coated in sweat, I look at myself in the mirror and realize that I'm smiling.

My cheeks turn pink when I orient myself and remember Kaius is in the room with me. I look at him, and an unfamiliar shyness overtakes me, as if I'm embarrassed for being so passionate.

Kaius stands up and his long legs carry him over to where I'm standing in a few steps. He cups my cheeks and his eyes flicker towards my lips, as if he intends to kiss me. His mouth parts slightly. The beginning of a word gets stuck in his throat. We stand there for a moment in silence. My chest is still heaving, but no longer from exhaustion.

"You are the most radiant creature I've ever seen. Never let anyone steal that from you. Least of all me."

He runs his hands from my cheeks to my neck, over my shoulders and down my arms until he takes hold of both of my hands. He places one of them on his shoulder and holds the other in his own.

He begins to slowly take small steps until we're turning in a circle together with me following his lead.

"I didn't think you could dance…or at least wouldn't care enough to learn," I say as his movements become more confident. Our feet and arms begin to sync until we're moving together as if we've been ballroom partners for years.

"I've lived a lot of lifetimes," is all he offers in explanation. "The reason everyone is so…happy today is because it's nearly the full moon. Every quarter-year, we like to celebrate our immortality with a feast and a ball."

My stomach turns at his use of the word *'feast'*. What else could that mean to vampires other than blood?

"I thought you were cursed...why would you celebrate that?"

"I *was* cursed," he confirms. "But not all vampires hate being immortal as I do. Where would their loyalty go if they discovered their King despises them?"

I nod in understanding and move on to my next question. "Why don't you celebrate on the night of the full moon instead?"

He's quiet for a moment as if pondering the answer himself. "Many vampires prefer to spend the full moon with their...lovers. It's when we're most powerful. When feeding gives us the most nourishment and strength and pleasure. When you've lived hundreds of years, sex tends to be the thing you use to feel human again...even if many of us wouldn't admit that."

"Oh," I say. I don't know why, but the sudden imagery of Kaius finding his pleasure in hundreds, if not thousands of lovers in the time he's been a vampire, has my heart aching.

"Would you like to accompany me tonight?" he asks quietly. If I didn't know any better, I'd say he seems...nervous. He flashes his teeth in a teasing grin. "I promise there will be food and wine for you there. Many vampires bring their human consorts with them."

I pause, letting my hands fall away from him and take a purposeful step back. "Is that what I am to you?"

"Adelasia, you know that's not what I meant."

"Actually, Kaius, I don't," I huff, my voice rising with my pulse. "You refuse to tell me why you kidnapped me. You refuse to feed on me. You refuse to do anything other than provoke me into asking questions you have no intention of answering. So you know what? No. I don't want to go to a stupid candlelit dance with you in this stupid, lifeless box you call a home. I don't want anything to do with you at all."

"Adelasia–" he calls after me, but I'm already three steps into the hall before he finishes the last syllable.

Twelve
Adelasia

My eyes burn with unshed tears, and I hate it. I hate that Kaius keeps me here with no evident reason. What have I ever done to deserve this? What is my crime? Dancing in the town center? Being in the wrong place at the wrong time?

I slam open my bedroom door and wipe the lingering sweat off my brow. Iphigenia is in the room, waiting near the bathroom with a fresh towel in her hand.

"Miss Adelasia, Lord Kaius has asked me to help you get ready for tonight."

"There's no need. Please leave."

"But—"

"I said get out!"

Iphigenia cringes at my tone, sets the towel down on the vanity, and leaves with her eyes glued to the floor. I feel bad for the poor girl. She didn't deserve the butt-end of my frustration, but there's no need for her to help me bathe or dress when I'm not going to this moonlight party the rest of them are so excited about.

I quickly change out of my leotard and tights, pulling on a long-sleeved beige tunic and a pair of fitted trousers. As I run my fingers through my hair to smooth out my bun, I realize as I look at myself in the mirror, that I look just like my mother. She often wore my father's old tunics when she worked on clothes or in the garden germinating the herbs and mushrooms my brother would bring home. She's always been a simple woman—giving her family so much while asking for so little in return.

I begin to feel a sense of shame. How much more comfortable could our lives have been if my parents hadn't sacrificed everything to keep me in dance school? How much more food would we have had on our table?

How much less would my father and brother have gone into the forest? And then it hits me, after all these years of denial.

It's my fault they died.

If I hadn't been a dancer, and we didn't have to hunt and gather for extra food and money, then the two of them would still be here. My passions, my ambitions, my desires are the reason they were in the forest that day.

When I turn away from the mirror, my dead pointe shoes sit on the edge of the bed. I use a finger to feel the worn-out satin and the fraying ribbons. I hold the shoes to my chest, and I watch as a tear falls from my face and lands on the fabric.

I choke back a sob as I turn and toss them into the fireplace, watching my life's purpose burn to ash before my eyes.

There's a biting chill in the air as I quietly make my way through the underground tunnels connecting the palace to the dungeon where Saddiq is kept. True to my word, I've brought him extra food, water, and clean clothing every day.

I don't usually linger for fear of Dravon finding me here–but today I am not afraid. Saddiq is shivering under a thin blanket when I sit in front of his cell, and he smiles when he sees me. He's missing another tooth, and a cut over his brow trickles blood into his eyes.

He makes a dismissive noise when he notices me looking at it. "Pay it no mind," he says with a soft grin. "It looks worse than it feels."

"You say that every day," I point out, sliding the provisions I brought through the enchanted door. Saddiq bows by touching his head to the dirty floor, even though I've told him a dozen times to stop.

He claims it's a mark of respect in his culture–that he could give me his neck and trust me not to step on it.

I always tell him that I don't deserve his respect, for I've done nothing but earn him beatings. No amount of food or water could erase that suffering.

"You've been crying," he points out quietly, biting into a crisp apple. When I look down but don't respond, he adds, "Did the Vampire King hurt you?"

"No," I say, and though Kaius is not on my list of favorite people right now, the thought of him hurting me seems preposterous. "I just had a funeral for my dance shoes, is all."

"The ribbon shoes?" he asks. He calls them that because the common tongue isn't his first language, and the proper word usually escapes him. "My daughter Habiba would find a fine friend in you. She would sing *'Baba! Baba! I want to dance for you!'*." He lets out a wistful sigh at the memory as tears gather in his eyes. "She would cut ribbons out of my shirts and tie them to her own shoes to pretend she was...oh, how you say?"

"A ballerina?" I ask.

He nods. "My wife Anya would scold me for allowing Habiba to ruin my shirts, but I never stopped her.

I would be gone for many long months, you see, hunting the demons and sending the money home for them. I never wanted her to feel like fabric meant more to me than her happiness. Oh, I wish you could meet her, Adelasia. She would never stop talking about how she met a real *balina*. We don't have such classes in Cambouri."

I give him a smile and a small laugh. "Your family is very lucky to have you. I hope one day to meet them."

Saddiq reaches through the cell door to take my hand in his. "I pray for it." He squeezes my palm. "Now tell me why you were really crying."

I give him a playfully annoyed glare, but I confess. "Kaius wishes for me to attend a celebration with him tonight...but I hate feeling like a pretty thing he gets to parade around at his leisure."

"Adelasia–" Saddiq says, squeezing my hand again, "Kaius holds you prisoner. You may not have chains as I do, but no man who steals a young woman from her life has pure intentions. I sense the heart in your chest is fragile. Do not trust the Blood King to handle it with care."

When I return to my room after ensuring Saddiq has everything he needs for the night, I begin to remove the pins from my hair, using the vanity mirror to brush out the lingering knots. In the reflection, I see a rectangular box sitting on the edge of my bed. I set down my comb, walk to the bed, and open the lid.

Inside sits a new set of pointe shoes. My mouth falls open in shock. I take the shoes in my hand and observe them. Imprinted on the shank is the same eight-pointed star that sits on my skin. They must be enchanted. I slip them on and rise up on my toes. They're incredibly stiff at first, but almost instantly, they wear to the perfect comfort for me.

I bite my lip to hold back a smile. I doubt Kaius knows I burned my other pair out of disdain for myself. I was ready to give up dance entirely because I felt I didn't deserve that joy anymore–but when I stand in these shoes, I can't help but feel that losing dance would only send me into further despair.

My arms wave at my sides gently, like a morning tide as I flutter from side to side at the foot of the bed. I even close my eyes to let my mind wander to a softer, warmer setting as I hum quietly to myself.

I bring myself back to reality and remove the shoes, vowing to sew ribbons to them once I finish my bath. I use my limited magic to fill the tub with warm water and dried lavender. I relax for a moment before using a washcloth to clean myself and rinse the day out of my hair.

After I drain the tub and fasten a robe around myself, I enter my room. Something cracks inside me when I step into the bedroom. The boxy, soulless walls have been changed entirely. Now there's elegant crown molding. The walls are still black, but the embellishments are a beautiful shade of gold that reflect the warm oranges and reds of the braziers. The old wooden bedframe is now equally ornate.

But most notably of all, on either side of the bed are two floor-to-ceiling windows. I cover my mouth as I gasp in awe at the first glimpse I've had of a sunset in a month.

I've never seen anything more magnificent. My eyes gloss over with a thin mist.

I stand at the window until the sun falls behind the horizon and the sky bursts into glittering stars and an admittedly beautiful moon.

"Do you still hate me?"

I jump at the voice behind me and turn. Kaius is standing near the door looking...splendid. His usual plain tunic and trousers have been replaced with black finery trimmed with silver embroidery. The feathered cloak he always wears truly makes him look like a king. His hair is loose around his face, but somehow it fits with the elegance of his attire.

I clear my throat, grab a comb and begin working through the non-existent knots in my hair. "I'd hate you less if you gave me a straight answer for once."

"Then ask me something, and I'll give you a straight answer."

I don't hesitate to ask, "What do you want from me?"

He crosses the room to take hold of my hand. He takes the comb, sets it on the vanity, and kisses my knuckles. "I want you to accompany me to the feast tonight."

I roll my eyes and tug my hand out of his grasp. I don't know why I expected anything different from him. I keep holding out hope only to end up disappointed every time.

"Adelasia...please. I–"

He reaches for my hand again and clasps his palm against mine, bringing our interlocked hands to his lips.

"I swear on my immortal life that there is *nothing* I want more on this night than to spend it at your side."

As soon as his words flutter into the air between us, a golden line appears, encircling both of our hands and wrists so that the pattern is only complete when our fingers are intertwined.

"What is this?"

"It's a vow," he whispers. "On my life. If my words at any point in the night become untrue, then the vow is broken, and I'll die."

My lips part as I hold up my hand in the space between us to examine the markings. If what he's saying is true, then the cost of his lie would be more than I can possibly comprehend. He's proving that I can trust him, at least in this. His vow combined with the thoughtfulness of his gift easily breaks through the lingering anger and disappointment I was harboring.

"Thank you...for my shoes. That was," I sigh and try my best to give him a genuine upturn of my lips, "very thoughtful."

I swallow the burning in my throat and rest my hand gently against his chest, carefully avoiding the ruby. "I'll attend the celebration with you," I concede. His hand squeezes mine, and the moment feels intimate, unlike anything we've shared before; even more than when he revealed his worst memory to me. "But there's one problem," I add.

"What's that?"

"I don't have anything to wear."

He chuckles in such a way that his fangs are on full display. "Are the dozens of dresses I had made for you not to your liking?"

"None of them match you. We wouldn't want to clash, would we?"

His face falls as if he's taken aback by my response. "I see."

He turns over his shoulder and motions behind him to reveal three dresses on mannequins. Each of them are striking, matching the black and silver details of his attire, with a matching feathered cloak.

The one on the left has a plunging neckline and long sleeves. The one in the middle is sleeveless with an elegant high neck and a keyhole between the breasts, and the one on the right is completely strapless and has a perfect sweetheart neckline.

I walk towards the middle one, calling to me because combined with the cloak, it's the least revealing. If I'm going to be at Kaius' side all night, I'd rather not draw more attention to myself. Especially since I have no intentions of letting anyone near my neck, having it exposed seems like I'd be asking for trouble.

"Dress. I will wait for you," he says softly, then leaves to wait out in the hall. I take a deep breath and shed my robe before slipping into the gown. A perfect fit.

I use magic to dry my hair, twisting it into a neat chignon at the base of my skull. I have no jewelry and no makeup other than a light pinkish balm for my lips, so I apply that and look over myself in the mirror.

I feel so...plain. Out of place. Like I don't belong here.

I suppose I don't.

I'm a human living in a palace full of vampires, and the only place I'll ever truly belong is strewn across the dinner table with fangs in my neck.

But somehow, I know that Kaius won't let that happen. Not tonight or any other night.

I fasten the cloak to my shoulders and when I open the door to meet Kaius in the hall, Cassius has joined him, coiled around his right arm. Cassius perks his head up when he sees me, as if in approval.

And Kaius...well he seems as disappointed as I felt looking into the mirror. I take a step backward, tears of humiliation welling up in my eyes when Kaius uses a finger to lift my chin.

"I am so jealous of the sun," he whispers.

"Why?"

"Moonlight is just reflected sunlight, which means the sun gets to admire your beauty twice as much as I can." He runs a knuckle along my cheek. "It gets to caress you, to kiss your cheeks and warm your skin." He sadly chuckles. "How can I compete with that?"

"I didn't realize you were competing with the sun for my affection."

"Neither did I," he whispers, as if it's a secret we now share. He holds out an elbow for me to take, to escort me to the celebration. Cassius is still tightly wrapped around his other arm. I've never known snakes to be affectionate creatures, but I also have never understood magic and how casually one wields it either. Kaius uses it as an extension of himself, and I often find myself curious about what that kind of power feels like and how it might have changed him through the years. I can't imagine sharpening a skill for centuries upon centuries as he has.

Of all the power that he's shown me, there must be more he has yet to reveal.

Does he do that for my sake, or his own?

"You're nervous. I can smell your terror," Kaius says, breaking through my racing thoughts.

"Normally you keep me hidden away from other vampires, and now you're taking me right to them."

I wish I could ask him why, but I know he'd only return a non-answer. The only thing keeping me at his side is the vow he made earlier. Surely someone with the wisdom a thousand years gives wouldn't make such a pact lightly, nor would he risk something so permanent if he didn't mean it.

Kaius leads me to the other side of the palace, where a large ballroom is already bustling with chatter. In the background, unsettling notes on stringed instruments vibrate throughout the hall, and it makes me feel like a lamb being led to slaughter.

As Kaius leads me through the crowds of red, hungry eyes, they simply nod in greeting as we pass. Their eyes stay fixated on me with chilling smiles, like they know a secret I don't. Like they're waiting for their king to give them permission to finally taste me.

The scene within the ballroom isn't as gruesome as I imagined it would be. There aren't human sacrifices laid out on the tables and there isn't the pungent metallic smell of blood in the air. Candelabras burn strategically around the room to light it enough for poor human eyes to see clearly. The ceiling is red-tinted stained glass, and it's no wonder this chamber has always been sealed tightly when I tried to enter it before. Other than the windows newly added to my suite, this is the only glass in the entire palace.

Kaius leads us to a table that's been set just for us. There are only two chairs, one significantly more ornate than the other, obviously meant for him. To my surprise though, he insists I sit there while he takes a seat in the smaller, more plain chair. Dravon immediately comes to greet him with a golden goblet of wine.

"My Lord," he says casually holding up his wine in toast, suspiciously eyeing me in the seat at his side. Kaius gently clinks the rims together. "A toast to your most lovely...*guest*."

I stupidly meet Dravon's feral eyes, and suddenly the cloak fastened around my shoulders and neck feels far too tight and suffocating. I touch my hand to my throat to attempt to relieve some of the pressure, but that only makes it worse. Kaius uses a dismissive nod to send Dravon away, and then he turns slightly to face me.

He reaches across the small space between us and unfastens the cloak from around my neck, letting it fall over the arms of my chair. Instantly, I can breathe better.

"Thank you," I whisper.

"You look like you're going to be sick."

I turn my head and glare at him. "You sure know how to make a woman feel beautiful." He simply smirks in response, and my eyes find Dravon across the room. "I don't like that one," I admit quietly, afraid he'll hear me.

His eyes float to Dravon too, and he leans over to be closer to me as if we're simply gossiping. "I've warned him that you are off limits."

I give him a sardonic scoff. "Is that supposed to make me feel better? You've claimed me, is that it?"

"Adelasia, please don't," he says, and if I didn't know better, I'd say he sounds almost like he was begging. "I brought you here because I thought the music and dancing would make you happy."

I ignore him and let my eyes continue to search the room. A human servant brings me a plate of turkey and small potatoes seasoned with rosemary and lemon butter. Some of the help and other humans have lightly bleeding fang marks at the curve of their necks, though they don't seem bothered or in pain. In fact, they seem proud.

"Do the humans really enjoy being fed on, or is that a lie your kind has spread to lure us in?" I ask.

"Yes and no." He motions his head towards a couple–both women, one vampire, one human. The vampire licks along the human's neck before biting. The human woman's face twists painfully for a few seconds, then her entire body relaxes. Her face quickly melts into an expression of very obvious pleasure. She's enjoying it.

"See how she licks her neck before biting? Our saliva acts as an aphrodisiac, to make humans less resistant. Something as simple as a kiss could flood the human mind with lustful thoughts. So yes, they enjoy being fed on, but their willingness? Questionable in certain circumstances."

My cheeks turn bright red as I watch the couple. They're touching each other and grinding their bodies together. The human moans softly, undeterred by the attention their display is bringing. I feel like I'm intruding, yet I can't look away.

I've never been touched by anyone other than myself. I've always been so concerned with my dance career that relationships and intimacy just weren't priorities for me. I've been on no dates, and I've only shared a kiss with one man in my entire life. He was my dance partner my first year at the company. It was a sloppy, uncoordinated kiss. He was a pleasant man, but there were no romantic feelings between us. The kiss was a quick moment after a show, and we never spoke of it again. Watching people be so open with their sexual desires is as intriguing as it is foreign to me.

"Adelasia," Kaius says softly, pulling me out of my trance. "Your dinner will get cold."

I nod and spend the next few minutes focusing solely on my plate, eating the entire thing and then even asking for seconds.

"I'm glad to see you're eating," Kaius says as I eat the last few bites. "I was afraid you'd starve yourself to spite me when we met."

"I thought about it," I admit. I lift my goblet to drink some wine to wash it down, but my cup is empty. I reach for a decanter placed between us to pour more, but Kaius places his hand over the top and gently forces me to set it down.

"Not that one," he explains, then waves over a servant who pours me a glass from a separate decanter.

I drink heavily for the next few hours, let the wine soak into my bones and allow my body to hum with a warm serenity. Some of the chatter has quieted down as the vampires find their own meals around the room. Soft cries of pleasure have filled the space, but through the influence of the wine, it no longer bothers me.

The music has turned a bit more melodic, and after a few moments of people-watching, Kaius offers me his hand. "Would you like to dance?"

I don't know if it's the drink or because I need something to do other than stare at vampires while they feed, but I don't hesitate, placing my hand in his.

Thirteen
Kaius

I lead her to the center of the room and pull her to my chest, closer than we were in the dance studio earlier tonight. I can feel her heartbeat spike at the proximity. She takes my hand and rests her other on my shoulder, and the action feels natural. She doesn't hesitate or falter when I take the lead. Her steps are perfectly in sync with mine, without a single hint of uncertainty on her face.

Adelasia is graceful, even under the influence of wine and her cheeks flushed red from witnessing the impropriety of others.

Her blood smells so alluring when she's blushing. Not mouthwatering like when she's scared, and not hypnotizing like when she's angry, but alluring. It doesn't make me want to feed, it makes me want to *protect*.

It frustrates me that she's not a cruel, malicious person like Yekaterina was. It would have made this last month so much easier. All she has wanted from the very beginning is to go home. After she told me the story about her father and brother, I felt worse for her mother, who has lost everyone she loves to demons.

Unlike me, Adclasia's thoughts do not seem to be of her home this night. Her captivating blue eyes are slightly dilated from the wine, but the solemn expression she so often has when she's around me is nowhere to be found.

As the song goes on, a smile graces her features and our steps become more elaborate, adding dips and turns that are done with such precision and speed that any other human would find themselves disoriented. Not her though. With each new step, her face grows more radiant with challenge. She's enjoying this—showing off her talent and technique.

I've been alive for a long, long time, and I've never seen anyone look more precisely confident than her when she dances. She puts the elegance of all other women combined to shame.

When the song ends, I have her in a dip so low the crown of her head nearly touches the floor. When I lift her back up, strands of hair have fallen out of her bun and now frame her face, some stuck to a thin sheen of sweat. Her chest heaves against mine, and we're so close I can almost taste the lingering soap on her skin from her earlier bath.

A small applause fills the room, and whatever thoughts were floating around in her head cease in that moment. She takes a step back from me and murmurs under her breath that she needs some air. I nod, and give her a few paces worth of space before I follow her out of the ballroom, down the hall, and out to one of the balconies overlooking the lower city of the valley.

I give her some physical space, lingering in the doorway. She looks over her shoulder to address me, but doesn't meet my eyes.

"You should go back to your celebration. I won't be long."

I approach her side and lean over the railing as she is, my hands clasped together with our shoulders and arms touching. "I'd rather be here with you."

She laughs quietly to herself at that, and my brow furrows. "What's so funny?"

"You'd have dropped dead if you lied to me just now."

I incline my head slightly. "Then it's fortunate that I was not lying." She looks back out over the railing and nervously picks at her fingers, zoning out towards the horizon. I brush my shoulder against hers to grab her attention. "Was it me?"

"Hm?" she hums in response.

"You ran away from the celebration for a reason. Was it me?"

"You wish," she teases humorlessly. Then she looks at me from under her lashes. "I was thinking about my mother. About how she's probably crying and alone right now while I'm dancing under the moon with a smile on my face."

I consider that for a moment, and then brush her shoulder again. "Write to her," I suggest. When she gives me a confused look, I say, "Write her a letter, telling her that you're alive. I'll get it to her."

"Really?" she asks hopefully, and I can hear the emotion getting caught in her throat.

"Really," I confirm. She looks as though she wants to ask if she can simply go home, but I think she understands well enough at this point that I would not allow it, even if she doesn't know why.

"Thank you," she whispers. "But you're scaring me with all this sudden kindness."

I smirk. "I can go back to being a cold brute if you wish."

She shakes her head. "You're not as cold as you want the world to believe."

"I was though, once," I admit. "I think you're overdue for a history lesson, Adelasia." She stays silent, waiting patiently while I contemplate how to tell her the truth without revealing her part in it.

"Do you remember when you told me that human legends believe that the vampires and the disappearance of the Tenth Priestess were related?" I ask. She nods. "I told you your legends are correct, but only partially. The Tenth Priestess was unfathomably powerful. She had an affinity for magic her sisters could not even begin to possess. She was...extraordinary. Cruel and malicious and ruthless, but extraordinary. She created the vampire race because she was bored one day and wanted to unleash her evil on the world."

"And...you were one of the first?" she asks.

"I was *the* first."

I watch as she does a calculation in her head, and then she gives me an expression of awe. "But that would mean you're a thousand years old."

I give her the slightest hint of a smile. "One thousand and fifty-eight. I was thirty-one when I was cursed. I was the only one the Tenth Priestess ever made before her death. Every vampire walking this earth is descended from me. I originally changed two others. Dravon is one of them, and that's why he's my closest advisor."

Her lip curls at his name. "What about the second?"

I tighten my jaw and continue without answering. "After I changed them, they created more vampires, and those vampires created more vampires and so on, but all of them lead back to me."

"That's why you rule them. They owe their immortality to you."

I nod. "Yes, but that's not the only reason. That man I killed in the kitchen? He was younger. Less than a decade as one of us. You can tell how young an immortal is by the hollows of their cheeks. The younger a vampire is, the more malnourished and sallow they appear, because they have not yet fed enough to become strong by vampire standards. Most vampires reach full maturity after about a century, if they even make it that long. The younger ones tend to stick together in their own clans out in the world and either get mauled by the werebeasts or cut down by demon hunters. If one gets killed, the rest fall."

"Why?"

"Because if you kill a vampire, every vampire descended from them also perishes."

The weight of my words and my earlier vow begin to settle on her shoulders. "So...if you died..."

"Then the vampire race would cease to exist."

This is not information humans should ever know. It's dangerous even, but I have trust in her that she will keep it to herself. I am finally opening up to her, after all. She's always wanted me to tell her the truth, and now I have. I don't think she'd do something to jeopardize that.

But as those thoughts enter and leave my head, I turn to her and notice she's crying. I feel a genuine concern in my heart and wipe away a tear, though they continue to spill faster as she turns her head away from me.

Her lip quivers as she finally meets my gaze, and she whispers, "You're going to kill me, aren't you?"

I pretend to be shocked at that conclusion, but the truth is, I'm not sure myself. "Why would you think that?"

"Why else would you tell me how to kill the entire vampire race if that knowledge wasn't going to just die with me?"

I take her wrist in my hand but she tries to tug it away. I grip it harder and force her to keep her gaze locked with mine. "Everyone dies, Adelasia. Eventually."

She scoffs. "Yes, you're right. Everyone dies. After they live full lives and...and...and get married and have babies or spend their entire adult life working towards being a professional dancer. Nobody deserves to die alone in this depressing, empty marble cage!"

I match her outburst with one of my own. "Dying in a marble cage is *nothing* compared to the millennium I have endured alone."

She roughly pushes away from me. "How many other unsuspecting women have you stolen from their lives in a thousand years? Hundreds? For what? Because you're lonely? Because you like your meals frightened? Does the despair make us taste better?"

"No. But *silence* does," I say coldly, before turning my back to her.

"Maybe you deserve to be alone," she says to my back.

I turn to her, my gaze filled with enough fury that it causes her to stumble backward. "You think I chose this life? You think I wanted to become a monster? You think I enjoy this life of eternal punishment?! I was cursed because I foolishly gave my heart to a cruel mistress incapable of loving me back. She wanted my devotion, but my heart was too much. It disgusted her. So when she grew tired of my simpering at her feet and worshipping the ground she walked on, she turned me into a monster. She watched me slaughter my own mother and had the gall to tell me it was better this way."

Her anger suddenly dissipates.

"It was the Tenth Priestess? She was the one you loved?"

"Yekaterina," I whisper. It's been centuries since I've said her name out loud. I don't like the evil that lingers in the air with it.

At the admission, Adelasia softens and steps closer to me. Her proximity brings me some peace and the rage within me begins to subside.

"I'm sorry," she offers gently.

"Don't be. I don't deserve nor want your pity."

"It's not pity," she argues. "It's empathy."

"Empathy is just pity in disguise."

"I've never met anyone more stubborn than you," she says, nudging her head against the sleeve of my coat.

"I have. *You*."

She playfully scoffs. "I am not stubborn!"

"It must be nice, living in such delusion."

She tries to shove me teasingly, but I catch her wrists in my hands. Her mouth parts slightly, like she's forgotten how quick I am compared to her. Her delicate fingers trace along the filigree details on my coat, and when she meets my gaze from under her lashes, her blue eyes look more vivid than I've ever seen them. It's like new life has taken place there. I could not recall the color of any other human's eyes in this palace even if my life depended on it.

But hers? I could never forget them, not even if I lived another thousand years.

"Stop it," I warn.

"Stop what?"

"Looking at me like that."

She blinks. "How am I looking at you?"

"Like I'm not a monster."

She lets out a shaky breath, and still staring into my soul, she says, "Ask me nicely."

I feel something shift inside me at her request. Like a small crack in my chest, allowing something to seep out of the very essence of who I am.

The black line intertwined with her golden vow begins to burn, and my hand begins to tingle ever so slightly.

This doesn't make any sense. That line does not belong to her. It's the remnants of a fate I abandoned long ago and a fate that she is not supposed to be destined for.

I close my eyes for a moment, and my jaw tightens as I loosen my grip on her wrists. "Please have mercy on my immortal soul, sweet Adelasia."

When I open my eyes, she's still gazing into the darkest, deepest parts of me. She finally breaks the gaze, only to meet it once again. "What color were your eyes, before you became a vampire?"

I think about it for a long time. Longer than anyone should think about that answer. I feel my face fall at the sad realization, and admit, "I can't remember."

"Kaius..." Adelasia whispers, freeing one of her wrists from my grasp to gently caress my cheek. "If there were a way for me to help you break this curse, I would."

Out of all the things she could have said to me at this moment, that's probably the one I wanted to hear the least. I take an abrupt step away from her, severing any lingering contact.

"We should go back," I prompt emotionlessly. "We'll miss the best part of the night."

I don't wait to see if she follows before I leave the balcony, and these conflicting feelings, behind me.

Adelasia does end up following me back to the hall where the celebration is being held, though she gives quite a wide berth between us. I stop in the center of the room, and she joins me a few seconds later. I nod my chin upwards to prompt her to look. As she does, the moon reaches its crest right above the enchanted red glass ceiling.

The moonlight filters through the mural, creating a stunning aurora above our heads in warm shades of red, orange, yellow, and pink. Small specks of the aurora fall to us, dusting her cheeks like freckles and her raven-black hair like gemstones.

"What is this?"

"Moonlight," I answer. "To remind those of us who long for the sun that there's beauty even in the deepest part of the night. When you live for hundreds of years, sometimes you need the reminder."

"Is it really so bad? Being immortal?"

I circle her until I'm standing behind her. I carefully pick out the pins holding her hair in place to let it fall down her back, and then trail my hands up her scalp, tangling my fingers into her hair. She lets out an uncertain sound of pleasure at the feeling.

"We gain strength and apt senses, yes, but think about everything we lose. Everyone we've ever known as a human will eventually grow old and die. We can never taste our favorite foods again. We'll never feel the warmth of the sun. You'll reach a point in your immortal life where you can't even remember what your own eye color was before you were turned. If we are religious, then we lose our connections to our deities because they believe us to be abominations. We'll never see a full sunset or sunrise again. We can't have children, and if we had children before we turned, they're unable to survive the change themselves. We lose so much more than you can even comprehend, Adelasia."

I feel the sharp rise and fall of her shoulders. She's crying. I nudge her temple with my nose and rub her arms with mine before wrapping her in a calming embrace. "You'd hate losing those things, wouldn't you?"

"That's not why I'm crying." She turns slightly to look up at me. "I'm crying for *you*."

I smile. "Don't waste your tears on me, Adelasia. I don't deserve them." I use my thumb to brush away one of the drops streaming down her face.

After the initial awe from the ceiling wears off, the room grows quiet as people begin to leave. Adelasia and I are left alone under the filtered moonlight. My hand still caresses her cheek and I can see her heartbeat pounding wildly in her throat. The air between us is warm with delicious tension, and the rosy sheen of her lips is even more tempting than the smell of blood coursing through her veins. To resist the sudden and overwhelming urge I have to feel those lips pressed against mine, I take one of her hands and spin her around a few times until she's pressed into my chest in a dancing position.

"May I have one last dance?"

She smiles and teasingly rolls her eyes. "I think I liked it better when we were fighting all the time."

"We can go back to that tomorrow. Just give me this night to pretend otherwise."

We have no music, and no audience, but our dance isn't any less passionate as it was before. Dancing with her feels ethereal. She's so confident in the way her body moves. She needs so little direction from me that my presence here feels almost useless, but I wouldn't trade this moment with her for anything.

Not even...

I pause abruptly as she spins out of my arms and Adelasia's face falls. I swallow and stiffen my back. "It's late. Let me take you back to your room so you can sleep."

I can see in her face that sleep is probably the last thing on her mind right now, but I'm not giving her a choice. I can't think rationally when she's around, and this is not the time for me to lose my head.

I have to look away because I can't stand the disappointment on her face when she takes my arm and allows me to lead her out of the room. The walk to her suite is silent, with only the tap of her light footsteps filling the halls. When we reach our destination, she turns to face me again.

Despite my better judgment, my trembling, still tingling hand brushes a loose strand of hair away from her cheek before I trace the angles of her jaw with my forefinger. When I reach her chin, I use my thumb to feel the fullness of her bottom lip. I hear her stop breathing.

A low growl emanates from deep in my throat before I drop my hand from her face.

"Goodnight, Adelasia," I whisper as I turn my back to her and slowly retreat down the hall. With each step I take away from her, I grow more and more frustrated at the knowledge that I haven't heard her door open. She's still in the hall, watching me walk away from her.

I stop walking and drop my head in defeat, and that's when I notice the golden vow line on my hand is glowing still, and the black one seems to be throbbing in sync with her heartbeat. With all the enhanced speed my curse of vampirism gives me, I'm standing in front of her again in an instant, so quick it causes her to gasp and step backward into her bedroom door.

"Damn you," I whisper, before gently grabbing her throat and pulling her lips to meet mine. She lets out a sound of shock, but quickly meets my fervor with her own. Her hands fist themselves into my coat as she pulls me deeper into her. She melts into my embrace, practically going weak at the knees.

When I break the kiss to let her breathe, the gravity of what I've just done devastates me. Without saying another word to her, I walk away.

And this time, I keep walking.

I find myself in my private study among old, dusty tomes and candles that haven't been lit in centuries. I hardly ever come in here, only when I need absolute silence and a place to think.

I flop into my large wingback chair and prop my feet up on the black marble desk.

The dagger that has become both my salvation and my worst enemy in the past few hours sticks out of my boot. I take it from its sheath and hold it by the blade in my hand, examining it carefully.

I sigh quietly to myself. "What have I done?"

Kissing Adelasia is one of the worst sins I've ever committed.

Now she'll feel rejected at the first hesitance of any further affection, and what's worse, is if she wasn't already growing attached, she certainly is now.

I take it back, the worst part is that she doesn't even know why she feels a pull between us, but I do—and it's not for the original purpose of her presence in my life.

What a mess.

I can still feel the softness of her lips against mine. I can still feel the passion and I can still hear the soft sigh of pleasure when she melted into me. I can still see the desire in her eyes asking me to do it again before I walked away. It's woven in the deepest part of my thoughts.

And with this damned vow on my skin still golden, even she knows she's still on my mind. She's been engrained there since I met her. She's burrowed her way into my soul and now I've developed...*feelings*. Feelings I *shouldn't* have for the only thing keeping me from earning my mortality back.

One more night.

That was all that was supposed to be standing between me and the only thing I've wanted for the entire millennium I've been living with vampirism. Now I've gone and added a kiss to that equation.

I've never known myself to be so stupid.

"Cassius," I call out softly. "Are you in here?"

I don't look away from the dagger as I wait a few moments. Cassius slithers up the side of the desk and coils himself on the edge.

"Tell me what to do," I beg. "I can't be trusted to make wise decisions when I can still feel her lips on mine."

Cassius' tongue flickers out. I narrow my eyes at him. "Don't give me that look. I didn't intend for it to happen this way! I just wanted her to enjoy her last night!" I rub the bridge of my nose as if I have a headache, though the ailment doesn't manifest itself in vampires. "It's her fault. She makes it hard to hate her. She's the furthest thing from that wretched soul she's hosting. It's...it's not fair." I glance at Cassius. "I should just kill her in her sleep and get it over with."

The limbless reptile companion I've known for hundreds of years has never been one to show any emotion other than aloofness. Rarely does he show signs of anger or irritation.

But what I see in his eyes when I utter that sentence is nothing short of pure, unfiltered fury. He tenses and opens his mouth to show me his fangs. His white eyes peer straight into my black soul, and for the first time in the centuries I've known him, I feel threatened.

I open my mouth to defend myself from his wrath, but I suddenly feel like my chest has collapsed. Like the weight of the world is pressing down. I rub my sternum with my palm, and the ghostly feeling of an unbeating heart beginning to pound resonates within my chest. It's like some force has restarted my petrified heart. Cassius slithers away from me and out the door quicker than I've ever seen him move.

And then I realize I've known this feeling in a past life.

Panic. Anxiety.

Adelasia!

Fourteen
Adelasia

I can't sleep.

I can't stop thinking about Kaius. I can't stop thinking about the way he kissed me, or about the very real possibility that a vampire has feelings for me.

Or the very real possibility that I might have feelings for him, too.

Why else would I let him kiss me? It can't be because I'm lonely here. I've never craved intimacy from a man before, not even something as innocent as a kiss.

Though, our kiss wasn't exactly chaste. It was passionate and warm and addicting. I didn't want to stop kissing him, and though he walked away from me, I know he didn't want to stop either, because the golden line on my arm is still perfectly intact.

I toss and turn in my bed trying to will my mind to stop thinking about Kaius. I settle on my side, and I focus on the quiet of the room and the crackle of the fireplace. I focus on their warmth until it lulls me into that limbo between wide awake and asleep.

And then I hear the door creak. I stay on my side, pretending to sleep, but I can't help the smile that creeps to my cheeks.

He came back for me. Even if it's just to check on me, he came back. I'm sure he can hear my heart thudding wildly in my chest–giving it away that I'm awake and desperately want him to kiss me again.

I feel him come closer and closer, his footsteps nearly silent. A hand tenderly brushes along my cheek.

And then it flips me onto my back and clasps over my mouth. I gasp and try to make out the figure above me. When I realize it's not Kaius at all, but Dravon, I begin to panic and screech. All of it is to no avail. I know I have absolutely no chance to fight him off.

He shushes me, but it's in no way comforting. It comes off as a hiss more than anything. He looks down at me with a wicked smile on his face and a raised brow, telling me without words that if I'm quiet, he'll let me go.

His eyes look demonic and more unsettling than usual, like there's a cloud of malice in them.

After a few more useless attempts to buck him off, I stop fighting. He releases my mouth and sits back a bit.

"What do you think you're doing?" I gasp, trying to back away from him, though I have nowhere to go except closer to the headboard.

Dravon grabs my jaw and squeezes until it feels like my bones are about to crack under his ruthless grip. Then he moves my head from side to side to examine my neck as he's done before. He scowls. "Why hasn't he fed on you yet?"

I scowl back. To that, he smirks. "Unless…he's been feeding…elsewhere," he murmurs as he lets go of my jaw to run his hand down the front of my nightgown. I shove his hand away and then smack him.

My bravery quickly turns to fear when he backhands me so hard that it knocks me from the bed to the floor. I groan in severe pain as I sit up, trying to reorient myself. My hand goes to my cheek, and I feel a warm wetness there. I look at my fingers and find blood.

I look up at Dravon, now standing over me as I sit dazed and confused on the ground. He examines a ring on his middle finger and licks my blood from it. That must have been what cut me.

He lets out a pleasurable groan and then smiles. "You taste…so good," he growls as he pulls me to my feet by my elbow. I stumble around, colliding with the wall to hold myself up. My blood still drips down my cheek, and he turns ravenous at the sight of it. His eyes turn black, his fangs grow longer, and before I even have time to react, they're digging into the tender flesh of my throat.

I do the only thing I can do: I scream.

Though it doesn't last for very long, because just as Kaius told me earlier tonight, the pain doesn't last long. It's quickly replaced by...*warmth*. Pleasure. Euphoria. My eyes roll back as my body goes limp. I can't tell if it's from the sensation, or because I'm slowly falling unconscious from the blood being drained from my body.

The scary part is–I don't really care. The racing heat in my body won't let me think about anything else. As I am teetering on the dangerous edge of consciousness, Dravon makes a noise of shock before he releases me.

He stares at me, wide-eyed as my blood drips down from the corner of his mouth. My hand clasps the bite at my neck as I watch Cassius slither up Dravon's back to peek over his shoulder at me.

Then Dravon falls to the floor, his eyes still aware, but his body unable to move. Paralyzed. Cassius must be venomous to demons.

I sink to the ground with my back still against the wall, breathing heavily, still on the verge of passing out. Cassius lightly nudges my leg as if to tell me it will be okay.

Kaius bursts through the door then, with so much urgency and conviction that it breaks free from the hinges and the iron lands on the ground with the metallic clang.

His eyes meet mine and he rushes to me, crossing the room quicker than my human eyes can comprehend. When he reaches for me, that's when I break down. I fall into his embrace and sob incoherently, clawing at him.

"Kai...Kaius please...*help me.*"

I desperately beg and plead at him, but he simply kneels next to me looking perplexed. I grab him by the front of his shirt and pull him close to me so we're face-to-face, our foreheads touching as I look at him from under my wet lashes.

"Kaius *please* help me. I don't want to be a vampire."

I manage to get out my full sentence before I completely break down again.

"Adelasia," Kaius coos. "Adelasia, look at me." I sniffle and whimper as he forces my eyes to meet his again. "You're not going to be a vampire. I promise."

"But...but..." I stutter as my hand goes back to touch my neck. I can see Kaius struggling with his own bloodlust at the sight. His eyes flicker from red to black and then back to red. He opens and closes his mouth as if his fangs are aching and causing him immense pain.

He doesn't say another word until he lifts me into his arms and cradles me to his chest. I shake and cry quietly into his embrace as he carries me out of the room to his own. A few minutes later, he gently deposits me on a marble countertop next to a basin of water and some rags.

I flinch when he moves my hair out of the way to look at the bite mark on my neck.

I swallow thickly, all of my energy going into forming a coherent sentence. "Can you…can you suck out the venom or something?"

It feels ridiculous to suggest it out loud, and that feeling only fortifies when Kaius' face twitches into a devilish smirk. He takes one of the rags and soaks it in the water basin before gently wiping away the blood on my neck.

"You're not going to turn into a vampire, Adelasia. There would be no humans left to feed on if all it took was one bite. How could we keep cattle if that were the case?"

I don't speak as I consider that. He's right, of course. If all it took was a single bite to turn humans into vampires, the human population would quickly dwindle until the vampire population became unsustainable.

Kaius stares at the cut on my cheek as he cleans my neck and then sighs. "You're going to be fine. I promise."

"Why did he attack me?"

Kaius again focuses on the cut across my cheek. "I suppose I'll be spending tomorrow trying to figure that out."

"What will you do to him?"

"Some light maiming, perhaps."

"I'm serious."

"So am I."

I gulp, and as Kaius wrings out the rag filled with my blood, I watch him struggle to control his thirst. His eyes grow darker by the second, his movements more rigid, his energy more dangerous.

When he lifts the rag to my neck to wipe again, I gently grab his wrist to stop him. His tense jaw flexes and his mouth quivers almost angrily as his now black eyes meet mine.

"Taste it," I suggest.

"Adelasia—"

"It's okay," I whisper. "Why let it go to waste?" I can feel the hesitation radiating off him in waves, clouded by desire and hunger.

He examines me for a moment, perhaps looking for fear or justification that this is a bad idea, but I can see the moment he finds none and allows himself to accept the invitation of this simple pleasure he gets to indulge in after all these weeks of resisting.

He cradles my head in his hand, and the other snakes around my waist to tug me closer to the edge of the counter so he's snug between my thighs. I feel his tongue drift over my neck, savoring every drop of blood still seeping from my slowly clotting wound.

I still feel lightheaded, so I let him fully support my head and neck with his hand. I simply slump forward, close my eyes, and focus on the way his tongue slides across my skin.

His tongue finally darts over the fang marks on my neck, and a sharp zing of pleasure darts from my neck straight down to my core. I feel him hesitate there at the existing fang marks, and I can feel his mouth twitch as he contemplates finishing what Dravon started.

I don't move or make a sound as I wait for him to decide what he wants. If it's to feed, then I will let him. I knew this would happen eventually, right?

It feels like an eternity before he moves. He brings his mouth even closer to my neck, and I close my eyes as I wait for the prick of his fangs, but they never come.

Instead, I feel him place a gentle kiss on my neck, and another on the line of my jaw. Another to the cut along my cheek. Then, he reaches my lips and gently kisses me. I open my mouth to let him softly explore, slow and languid.

When he finally breaks the kiss, I open my eyes to find him already staring at me. I watch the thick lump travel down his throat as he swallows.

Still catching my breath, I let my hands trace up and down the fine details of his coat. "Can I ask you something?"

He nods, setting the rag to the side, still standing between my parted legs. His long arms rest on the countertop next to my thighs. The fabric of my nightgown sits high on my legs, and I feel his thumbs brushing across the lace hem. His cold fingers bring goosebumps to my skin.

In truth, I have more than one question. Hundreds, even, and many of them start with 'why'.

But I settle on something seemingly more simplistic.

"What does it feel like to crave blood?"

"Agony," he answers. I quietly scoff at his one-word answer before he elaborates. "What's your favorite scent, Adelasia?"

"Um...peaches, I suppose."

"Then imagine you're starving. You're nauseous and shaky and irritable. Then the smell of fresh, ripe, juicy peaches wafts from another room. You'd be inclined to search for them, yes? And then when you finally see them, your mouth begins to water, you begin to fantasize about how satisfying that first bite will be. Now imagine you finally get to taste one, and you're so hungry that you can't even enjoy it. Then, when it's gone, you realize it wasn't satisfying at all. The hunger is still there, consuming your every thought, and so you eat another because you're convinced you're just not full yet. That one doesn't sate the hunger either, and on and on it goes until you're nearly weeping for relief that you know will never come."

"If that's true, why didn't you finish what Dravon started?"

"*Feeding* and *tasting* blood are two different things," he explains. "We feed by siphoning blood through our fangs. Tasting is...well, I've already explained what it does to humans and vampires. It's an outlet for pleasure only. It provides no sustenance, no nutrition, but that's not to say it isn't any less delicious."

"So you liked it then? My blood?"

"*Liked it*?" he retorts, pulling me even closer to the edge of the counter so he can easily lean down to whisper in my ear, the very tip of his index finger on his right hand tracing up the inside of my thigh. "You cannot fathom the thirst currently residing in my throat for you."

I swallow the rock in my own throat. My heart begins to race with every inch his finger travels over my leg, up and down and back up again. Despite how cold his fingers are, the touch lights my skin on fire. My body tingles in places no man has ever touched before, and there's a part of me, mostly between my legs, that's begging Kaius to touch me there.

Maybe even taste me, too.

"Do you remember the first night I was here, when you said that fear makes my blood taste better?" I ask as he traces his nose up the side of my neck.

"*Vividly.*"

I gulp. "What do you think desire makes it taste like?"

I feel him smirk against my throat. "Peaches."

I scoff, and it gets cut off with a hiss when he lightly nips at my neck where Dravon bit me, though not enough to sink his teeth into me. His fingers travel further up my thigh, so high that I know he can feel the heat gathered at my core.

I find the courage to meet his eyes, and all I see in them is pure lust. Lust for my body and my blood, and I can't tell which he wants more.

The black depths of his eyes used to scare me, but I see so much of him in them now. Now instead of unholiness, all I see is uncontrollable vulnerability. Uncontrollable need.

Achingly slowly, he moves his finger to gently rub along my core over my thin underthings. It's tingly and warm and the light touch of his finger has my body silently begging for more. I wonder if he can smell it like he can smell my blood.

My thighs tense as he rubs the pad of his finger in circles around the most sensitive part of me. My mouth falls open, and I quietly sigh. Each circle feels so sickeningly sweet. I shouldn't want this, but I do. I want this and more.

I want *him*.

Shamelessly, I grind my hips against his finger, forcing his touch to become firmer. He licks his teeth and smiles as if he's been waiting for that.

"Let me taste you, Adelasia. Just one more time."

I gulp before slowly nodding, tilting my head to the side to give him access to my neck. He smirks, still rubbing me in soft circles. He stops only to have his hands glide up the outside of my thighs to wrap his cold fingers around my underthings. He slowly, so slowly, pulls the garment down my legs, never once letting his eyes leave mine. If he's searching for hesitation, he won't find it there.

My forehead crinkles with confusion when he kneels before me, still not letting his eyes drift from mine.

"What are you doing?" I gasp.

"Tasting you," he purrs, placing gentle kisses to the inside of my thigh in a line until he reaches my sex, which is now thoroughly weeping for attention.

"I...I thought you meant–"

"Silly girl, do you think I can't multitask?" he murmurs against the most intimate part of me, his words dancing over the sensitivity there.

"Kaius I've never—"

His middle finger inches closer and closer to me. When the pad of his finger touches my bare center, I throw my head back and suck in a sharp breath at the sensation.

I feel a slight pinch and a sting. I look down to see Kaius has used his fang to cut my skin right above my core. He lets a small drop of blood gather before he sensually licks it up, trailing his tongue up to my navel and then kissing back down my stomach without breaking eye contact.

The pleasure that surges through my veins sits deep in my core, begging for more. He lets another drop of blood gather and trail down my sex, and only then does he lick up the drop. The action is sinful and erotic and my heart begins to beat faster. My skin grows flushed. My eyes grow heavy.

His tongue slides between my folds and he circles it around the bundle of nerves just below the cut before tasting both my blood and arousal in one swipe.

"Delicious," he purrs against my skin. His mouth skillfully pleasures me while he greedily swipes up every drop of my blood that seems to drip faster the longer he devours me.

I feel a coil deep in my center begin to tighten, and my cries of pleasure grow more desperate as he slips his middle finger inside me. Between his mouth, his finger, and the way he groans with each pass of his tongue that tastes my blood, I fall apart. My body tenses and I throw my head back again as I convulse around his finger and experience a taste of the pleasure he's always told me I could find only in his world.

He licks along the cut one last time before standing abruptly and crashing his lips to mine. His hands go to the straps of my nightgown—mine go to his cloak to shove it away from his shoulders until it falls to the floor. My perky breasts spill over the top of my gown as my hands unbutton his coat.

His hands leave my body to unlace his pants, but something in his energy shifts in the opposite direction. We're both half-dressed, but I no longer see desire in his eyes.

I see that hardened, emotionless wall I've spent these weeks slowly breaking through.

Without a word, he tenderly lifts the straps of my nightgown back into place, covering my chest with the fabric, and then steps backward to remove himself from the cage of my legs.

"Kaius—" I plead in an attempt to hold onto the moment before it's gone completely, but he holds a finger up to my lips and shushes me. He takes my hand in his to help me down from the counter. There's something...shameful in the downturn of his mouth.

"Your neck will bruise by morning. I'll bring a salve for the cut on your cheek to help the swelling. You can sleep here tonight."

He leads me to his bed where he settles me under the blankets and even takes care to tuck me in. He sits at my side and uses a gentle finger to brush away a strand of hair and trace down my jawline.

"Did Dravon say anything to you before he attacked?"

The sting of rejection must be very clear in my eyes. I can feel the pathetic tears ready to spill over, but he does not seem to care.

I shake my head.

"Are you sure?"

"I...I remember thinking his eyes looked strange. But Kai–"

He cuts me off with a nod. A sign that he doesn't want to hear more. He stands without a word, and I lunge for his arm, fisting my fingers into the sleeve of his shirt.

I gulp through the ache in my throat. "Kaius. Stay. Please."

He lets out a long exhale, before roughly tugging himself away from my grip, all of his earlier care and gentleness gone.

And then he leaves the room, but more importantly, he leaves me feeling lonely, confused, and heartbroken.

Quiet tears continue to spill from my eyes, shame and humiliation flowing freely. I wipe my face just as I notice Cassius slither onto the bed, slowly making his way towards me. I lie down and turn on my side so he and I can be nose to nose.

His eyes scream intelligence, and though I wish Kaius was here with me, Cassius is good company too.

"Thank you for stopping Dravon," I say quietly through a sniffle. Cassius' forked tongue flickers out, touching my nose. I blink rapidly in confusion and interest. I sit up slightly, and Cassius follows my action. "Can you understand me?"

His tongue flickers out again, and I settle back on my side.

"Will you stay with me?" I ask. Cassius then curls into a spiral at my stomach, and I take it as a yes. I stay silent for a few moments, and then look at him again, my lip quivering. "What did I do wrong?"

Cassius perks his head up at my question, pauses for a moment, and then moves his head slowly from one side to the other, as if to say *'nothing'*. I don't believe him, and so I bury my face into the pillow, which only makes me cry harder because it smells like the only person I want in the world right now—Kaius.

Cassius comes closer to me, winding himself around my wrist. A line of scales all the way down the center of him turns from pitch black to shimmering gold. When he lets my wrist go, I look to find that there's a golden line circling it. A vow.

I compare it to the one on my other arm; the vow Kaius made to me. It's still golden, too. I tuck my hands under my pillow and sigh. "I don't know what promise you've made, but I trust you."

I swear I see a smirk on the corner of his mouth, before he lowers his head and tightens himself in a coil again. I take one last peek at the golden lines on my arms, and drift to sleep.

My dreams are filled with visions of a white-eyed, dark-haired, white-winged man standing next to Kaius and me.

His gaze on us can only be described as unbearable longing.

Fifteen
Kaius

Dravon is still deathly still on the floor of Adelasia's suite when I come for him. His eyes are open, wide with confusion and shock when I stand over him.

"Lord Kaius..." he whispers.

I hold up a finger in warning to hold his tongue. "You will tell me what happened, and you will tell me now."

As he opens his mouth to respond, I see that fog cast over his eyes. It's subtle, but once it's noticed, it's hard to ignore. I squat down to look closer, and it's gone.

"I wasn't in control," he gasps, and in all the time I've known Dravon, which is the entirety of my immortal life, I've never known him to look...distraught. Worried. Scared.

It unsettles me to my core.

"Clearly," I mutter. "I seem to recall telling you several times that Adelasia was *not* to be touched by your insatiable thirst. I've killed our kind for calling her a liar. What should be your punishment for defying me? For *harming* her?"

Dravon whimpers. "I'm already a dead man."

"Don't be dramatic, the venom will wear off in a few hours."

"It's not the venom, Kaius."

I stiffen. Dravon has never, not once in one thousand and twenty-seven years, used my name. It's always followed by a '*Lord*' or replaced with '*sir*' or some other formality. Never just my name.

His eyes fog over, return to normal, and then fog over again. He begins to twitch, as if trying to thrash around while under the influence of the paralysis. He growls and grits his teeth.

I grab him by the lapels of his coat and shake him. "Tell me."

Dravon begins to panic, and when a fearless man begins to panic, so do I.

"Dravon!" I growl. "Tell me!"

He widens his eyes, and they flicker back to their normal glassiness.

"The Priestesses—"

His words are cut short by a thick wooden stake rising from the floor to stab him through the back, straight into his heart. His body goes through one thousand years of decay in a matter of a few seconds, and he falls to ashes on the black marble floor.

I catch myself with my hands as I fall backward slightly, staring at the stake as tall as I am protruding from the ground.

Dravon is dead, and he's been immortal for nearly as long as I have. He's got to have hundreds of thousands of vampires descended from him, and every single one of them just faded into dust.

I stare at that stake for a long while, contemplating his last words and what they could mean, and then it hits me. The fog cast over his eyes was the influence of the Priestesses, using him as a spy over my court.

And if Adelasia saw that fog over his eyes, then there is a very high possibility that the Priestesses now know of her existence.

They're coming to reclaim their sister when their magic is at its strongest. At the next full moon.

Tomorrow.

I use magic to repair Adelasia's bedroom and remove any signs of Dravon from the space. It takes not but a few seconds, and I spend nearly the entire rest of the night agonizing over the way she looked at me when I stopped letting myself *feel*.

I should have never tasted her. I should have never touched her. The more time I spend with her, the more I'm losing myself in her. She's on my mind all the time. She never leaves. I can smell her, I can hear her heartbeat, I can feel her presence and now I can *taste* her. Not only does she linger in my mind, but now she's all over my lips and my clothes and I'm wholly consumed by nothing but her.

I shouldn't have walked away from her earlier, and I know I hurt her in doing so. I can practically feel her heartbreak in my own chest through our shared magic.

I want her more than anything, and coming to that realization while I was with her scared me, because it comes with a choice I can no longer make.

I don't have the strength to.

Betrayed by my own heart once again, and I dread it more than I have ever dreaded anything before. She is tangled in one destiny that is dripping with blood and another that would ruin her as immortality has ruined me.

Adelasia, my sweet agony. My love is a poison on your lips. A curse far crueler than vampirism, destined to be the fated mate of a man whose life has been consumed by the desire to end yours.

When I return to my bedchamber, I step through the door to find Adelasia, thankfully, asleep. Cassius is in the bed with her. A ridiculous pang of jealousy shoots down my spine at the thought that he's stolen my place on the bed. *My* bed.

I toe off my boots and approach the bed and lightly flick the invertebrate coiled there. He lifts his head and hisses quietly, and that's when I notice the golden streak down his back and the golden line around Adelasia's left wrist.

I scowl at him. I didn't even know he could make vows. He can't even speak!

"Move," I whisper angrily. Cassius shows me his fangs as if in warning that he has no qualms about biting me as he did Dravon. He moves to the foot of the bed to make room for me, and I climb into the vacant space as slowly and quietly as I can.

I don't embrace Adelasia, but I lounge next to her, slumping slightly against the headboard as I watch her sleep. I use my magic to conjure a small jar of medicine for the cut on her cheek. I gather some on the tip of my finger and lightly run the balm along the cut to coat it.

The redness and swelling instantly begin to recede, and she sighs softly in her sleep at the relief. It brings a hint of a smile to my face. I don't like the knowledge that she's in pain, however minimal it might be.

I know when the night has reached an end and when the sun begins to rise, because the golden markings of my vow to Adelasia fade from my skin.

Vows have a way of knowing the truth, even if one is in denial about it. Perhaps I was a fool for wagering my life and the fate of the entire vampire race to prove my sincerity, but Adelasia wouldn't have believed me any other way.

She sleeps through the morning and well into the afternoon. In her time here, she's become more nocturnal simply because everyone else is. It pleases me to see her adjusting to this life, as temporary as it was always meant to be.

Vampires don't require sleep, but some do it simply for the routine. Immortality can get incredibly boring. When one has lived for as long as I have—read and witnessed all of history as it happened, traveled the world, learned every language and studied every culture, there tends to be little to do except contemplate the existential loneliness.

It's the thing I miss most about being a human. Humans are always learning, always clinging to their life because they know their time on this earth is limited. There's no chance they'll get to experience everything the world has to offer, and that's why their lives are so precious to them.

Because *time* is precious to them.

When Adelasia stirs at my side, I sit up straighter. I wait patiently for her to open her eyes and orient herself. She looks at me in confusion and lifts her head from the pillow, examining the room for a moment before her focus comes back to me. Her hand reaches up to feel her neck, and she winces slightly at the tenderness of Dravon's bite.

"You came back," she whispers, unable to meet my eyes for longer than a second.

I smirk. "Someone had to make sure you weren't the first human to turn into a vampire from a simple bite."

My teasing doesn't bring brightness to her face as I thought it would, so instead, I change the subject.

"I am sorry for last night," I tell her.

"Which part?" she asks, and I can hear the pain in her voice.

"All of it," I admit.

Adelasia stands from the bed and I do so with her. I try to reach for her, but she steps back and then looks up at me. She's quiet for a long moment, and while she gathers whatever thoughts are in her head, I find myself staring at her lips.

I take a step closer to her and she doesn't recoil this time. I press our foreheads together and the smell of me lingering all over her excites me all over again.

"Why do you make it so hard to hate you, Adelasia?" I whisper against her lips.

"Maybe you're not meant to," she whispers back. "And I think that scares you."

I crave more of her, more than I allowed myself to take last night. More than I'm willing to take now and more than I ever should have taken in the first place.

"I may not know everything about your world, Kaius, but don't mistake me for a fool. I had the same vow on my skin, and I think you're not sorry at all about last night."

I don't like the way she's suddenly gained the ability to read me like an open book, and I find myself feeling defensive.

"You think I'm nothing more than a heartless, soulless, wretched monster. Why would I be capable of feeling anything for you?"

She doesn't back down from my challenge, and instead meets my poison with tenderness.

"I don't believe you're any of those things, Kaius. I think for the first time in a long time, you feel like you have something to lose." She uses her free hand to tenderly caress my cheek. I close my eyes and lean into it. "Tell me what it is you're so afraid of."

I knit my brows together as a physical pain shoots through my heart. "Everything," I admit quietly, and my shoulders slump inward in defeat, because I'm in too deep now. The truth is there, and she's going to pull it out of me, even if she breaks her own heart in the process.

"Tell me," she begs.

I feel...ready to weep. Fractured. I sigh and lift her chin so she has to look at me. I want to see her let me go and watch the betrayal flash across her eyes. I want to watch her hate me all over again, however painful it will be for me.

"Adelasia, I haven't felt my own heartbeat in centuries. It's grown cold from all those years of loneliness. You're the only thing in my life that makes me feel something other than despair. First, you gave me *hope*. Then you made me feel...alive, and in doing so stripped away that hope. I hate you for it."

I sink to my knees and tangle my fingers with hers. "I want to be a human again," I whisper. "I didn't realize until last night when I kissed you that my stolen mortality has never been my true curse. It's *you*, my sweet agony. We are bound by a cruel fate to fall in love, and you are bound by a cruel fate to end this curse of vampirism."

A single tear falls from her eye and I reach up to catch it with my thumb. "The scar on my back..." she whimpers, finally understanding why I've tried so hard to keep this from her.

"Adelasia, I am so, so sorry," I whisper up from my place on the floor. "I never intended for either of us to grow attached, and I didn't know until last night what we truly meant to each other."

"So that's the truth then? That I was a means to an end for you?" She shoves my hands away from her.

"Adelasia, please," I beg, finally standing and trapping her between my arms. "I wanted my mortality back so badly that I would have done anything to get it. But now—" I cup her cheek and turn her head to force her blue eyes to meet my red eyes. I sigh, my shoulders sinking in desperation at this impending heartbreak. "I'd live the rest of eternity as a vampire if it meant you got to experience the joy of a full human life that I never got to have."

She turns her head away from me, tears flowing freely now. "Breaking the curse isn't a ritual," she whispers, and then finds enough bravery to look at me. "It's a sacrifice." Her voice breaks when she adds, "You were going to kill me."

I shake my head. "Only in the beginning."

"Is that supposed to make it better?!" she shouts, trying to wriggle free of my grasp. "All this time I knew you would kill me, and you were too much of a coward to admit it to my face when I asked."

"I may be a coward, but there is no curse or cause that would lead me to harm you now. I swear it."

"You already have," she cries. Then, she attempts to shove me away. "Let me go. Kaius, let me go!"

When I don't yield, she does something I never imagined she would. She conjures a stake into her hand.

And I let her impale me in the chest.

Sixteen
Adelasia

Frantically, I run out of Kaius' room, passing servants and vampires alike as I rush through the maze of hallways until I reach the tunnels that connect the palace to the dungeon.

I reach Saddiq's cell and begin tugging on the iron bars with all of my strength. I use all the magic at my disposal trying to break through whatever barrier keeps him inside.

Saddiq notices the tears and how frightened I am, and reaches through the bars. He takes my face in his bony hands. His deep tan skin is so warm compared to the lifelessness of the walls around him, in both tone and temperature.

I continue to tug at the bars and grow increasingly more frustrated when I can't get him out. I need to leave this palace, *now*, and I won't leave Saddiq behind.

"We...we...we...we have to get you...out," I hiccup through my sentence, my mind rushing through a million thoughts at once.

"Adelasia, my kind savior, *breathe*," he tells me, and I mindlessly continue to pull on the bars until my strength fails me and I crumble to the ground in a fit of tears.

"We have to get out," I whine, pressing my cheek and forehead into the bars. "I don't want to die here."

A chill falls over the dungeon, and I find myself shivering as Saddiq tries to calm me down. He doesn't care to escape. His concern is for me, and I've never been more grateful for a friend in my life.

I curl into a ball as close as I can manage to Saddiq, and he sings a soft tune from his homeland that echoes off the walls of his cell.

"Adelasia," he says after he finishes his song, "You must make your escape now, before the night becomes too deep."

"I won't leave you," I protest.

"Listen. When you exit the valley, head to the East. Stay as close as you can to the edge of the Blackwood until morning. Only move deeper into the forest when the sun is out. At dusk, take shelter. Make no fires, and cover your waste so you do not attract the werebeasts."

I shake my head. "I won't leave you," I repeat.

Saddiq opens his mouth to say something, but we both go still and quiet when we hear the unnerving sound of chittering bouncing off the walls.

"What is it?" I ask. Saddiq quickly covers my mouth with his hand. The chittering grows louder—closer. I can't tell where it's coming from.

I want to run, to hide, but I can't leave Saddiq. The air around us grows colder and from the corner of my eye, I see that Saddiq and I are not alone.

But it's not a vampire that's come for me.

Seventeen
Kaius

I let the stake stay in my chest for a while. She barely missed my heart, and a part of me wishes she didn't. An even larger and more selfish part of me hopes she's just on the other side of that door, waiting for me to come to her.

But I know I will have no such luck. I don't deserve it. I don't deserve her. With the truth laid bare, she got to see what a monster I truly am, and how her intuition was right all along.

I grab the end of the stake and yell out in pain as I tug it free from my chest. Blood drips from the point, and

I let it drop to the floor before I stand. The wound begins to heal, and I walk out of the room.

At this stage in my immortal life, very little shocks me. I've studied magic for centuries, and thought I was a master in it, even if I didn't quite possess the power it takes to use it to its full potential.

I've always been certain of one thing, and that is that there is no magic that can raise the dead. Vampires are a special sort of magical being, and while we are considered undead, the process of raising a vampire begins in their human lives, so it's not affected by the natural limitations of magic.

If you stake a vampire in the heart, they're dead, and their body quickly decays to match their age, so many of us are left as nothing but bones or even dust when we die.

I certainly remember Dravon decaying into dust last night, so when I round the corner and see him standing before me, chest-to-chest, Adelasia momentarily leaves the forefront of my mind, and she's replaced with fear.

Something is not right, and I have a feeling he has Nine Priestesses to thank for his resurrection.

"You have guests," he hisses, and both of us have the same thought—only he beats me to it.

We both conjure stakes in our hands, but Dravon is just a bit faster than me, plunging his into my stomach, clean through to the other side.

I crumble to the ground with an incredibly painful groan, still recovering from Adelasia's stake.

"Play nice," Dravon warns. And there's nothing I can do as he grabs me by my arms and drags me through the halls, leaving a blood trail as he goes. He deposits me in the throne room.

I brace myself before I begin to tug the stake from my abdomen. Every minuscule movement feels like I'm being ripped open. The jagged edges of the stake leave micro-tears in their wake. Just as the stake is nearly out of my body, Dravon uses his boot to press it back down. I have no choice but to let him. I'm too weak to fight it.

I wince as I feel it tearing through me like razors.

"How are you alive?" I grunt. The pain is overwhelming, but I have too many unanswered questions to succumb completely to it.

"*Enemy of my enemy* and all that," he murmurs.

"Since when am I your enemy? You've been loyal for over nine hundred years! What changed?"

"*The times*, Lord Kaius. Someone has to take over when you're no longer King of the Damned."

Even through the pain, I can't help but roll my eyes. "That's what this is about? A throne?"

Dravon kneels and grabs me by the throat, lifting me slightly so we're face-to-face. "I knew you were a goner the moment I laid eyes on her. You're besotted. Infatuated. You've betrayed the vampire race at the very height of our power! I can't allow that. Not when your life is tied to the rest of us. With you out of the picture, I can usher us into a new age, a new millennium, where it is the *vampires* that rule this land, not the Coven."

"You imbecile! You think taking me out of the picture will make the Priestesses stand down from their absolute rule?"

"It was promised."

"Then you're a fool for trusting them. They will betray you the moment your usefulness has run its course! They will never give you what you want–it doesn't matter if it is your immortality or my throne. *You cannot have it.*"

"If I hand you and the girl over, I get to keep my immortality, and sit upon that throne and command a race you never cared to rule," Dravon sneers, pulling up his sleeve to reveal a golden vow line. "It. Was. Promised."

I grit my teeth and make sure he feels the fury in my stare. "Touch her again and it will be the last thing you do before you die for a third time."

Dravon sneers and leans even closer to me. "You cannot save her. Not from them."

For all the good it will do, I open my mouth to threaten him again, when the air turns putrid with the smell of the foul magic only the Nine Priestesses possess. It stinks of evil. Even the shadows seem to fear the shift in atmosphere.

Dravon lets me go, and I lie flat on my back, barely able to lift my head. The gem around my neck rumbles with the need to join its siblings in the hands of the Priestesses.

When I find the strength to lift my neck again, the Priestesses stand in a half-circle just a few steps away from my feet. Their long gray robes that cover them from head to toe float like a fog around their feet, billowing from the energy of magic. Their ornate headdresses glimmer with gems, precious metals, and other magical relics. Bones. Wilted flowers. Bloodstains.

Though they all look the same, it's easy to tell who they are by the authority they command simply by existing. Amatisi became their leader after I killed Yekaterina, and she's only grown more wicked as the centuries have passed without her sister. More wicked, and *far* less patient with me. We've never had a pleasant interaction, even when Yekaterina was alive. She always acted towards me as if she knew I'd be the downfall of their coven.

But Amatisi and the others don't understand that I never wanted to be their enemy. I only retaliated against Yekaterina for cursing me, and then they retaliated against me by cursing me again. *She* is the sole reason for our enmity.

Until I met Adelasia, I would have done anything to give them what they wanted in exchange for my mortality back. I would have sacrificed anyone; done any atrocities they asked.

I've always been desperate for freedom from my immortal prison, and the Priestesses know that better than anyone. They've used it to their advantage at every opportunity, but no longer.

I see Amatisi's head tilt downward to look at me sprawled out and injured on the floor. She snickers. "I do love it when a man greets me on his back."

Her voice sends shivers up the spines of even the most fearless men. It's feminine, but echoes with a demonic whisper that injects fear into the bravest of hearts. Her sisters say nothing. They stand there, unnaturally still and watch as Amatisi takes a step closer to me, close enough that I don't have to exert the energy to hold my neck up to see her.

"It's been too long, Lord Kaius. Three centuries, I think. Or has it been four? One tends to lose track."

"Not long enough," I mutter.

Amatisi begins to walk in a circle around my body. She makes a full rotation and then steps on my chest with her bare foot, adorned with golden chains and red paint.

"Where's the sacrifice?"

"I don't know what you're talking about."

Suddenly, I'm levitating in the air, face-to-face with Amatisi. My feet hover above the floor as she wraps her bony fingers with unnaturally long nails around the stake in my stomach. She rips it out, and I feel instant relief. She allows me one single moment of painless existence before she shoves the stake back into my stomach and lets me drop to the floor. I groan when my knees hit the cold marble and I hunch over, gripping the stake.

I pull it out again and brace my bloody hands against the floor, trying to hold myself up against the pain. Amatisi begins circling me again.

"Where's the sacrifice?" she repeats. I keep my mouth shut, grunting as I look up at the witch. She tilts her veiled head to the side, and though I can't see it, I can hear the smile in her voice.

"Oh, Kaius, you simply never learn, do you?" She takes a step towards me, her hand outstretched. From her fingers, dark magic begins to spread and swirl around me. "How many more centuries will it take for you to realize—" The magic solidifies into a collar of wooden spikes around my neck with a long chain attached. From behind me, sitting on my throne, Dravon pulls the chain, embedding the spikes in my throat. "—that it never pays to make an enemy out of me?"

Dravon snickers and pulls the chain again, embedding the spikes even deeper into my throat. The pain is almost unbearable. Amatisi uses her dark magic to put splintered wooden cuffs around my wrists, effectively rendering me useless.

Amatisi stops directly in front of me, tilting my head backward by my hair and then placing her thumbs on my temples. Her long, claw-like fingernails dig into my scalp.

"If you won't tell me what I want to know from your bleeding throat willingly, I shall take the knowledge from your weak mind by force," Amatisi purrs.

I know what's coming, so I use every last remaining shred of my focus and willpower to solidify a shield across my mind. If I let Amatisi invade my thoughts, it's over. Everything I have tried to protect Adelasia from will be out in the open.

My skull feels like it's being crushed when the magic enters my consciousness. Its sharp talons dig and scratch and scrape along the mental barriers I've put up. I can feel pain snake along my thoughts. Dravon must be pulling the chain, trying to get me to break my focus, but I will not. I've been alive far too long and endured far too much over the centuries to be so easily taken down by splinters.

I can hear Amatisi's voice in my head. She laughs. "What is it you're trying so hard to protect, Kaius? Is the sacrifice truly worth all this trouble?"

I grit my teeth and roar with frustration when I manage to push Amatisi completely out of my head. She tilts her head to the side, impressed by my fortitude. But she knows I'm breaking. If she tries to enter my head again, it's over. She'll know exactly where to find Adelasia and I'll have no way to protect her myself.

When Amatisi grabs my temples and invades the sanctity of my most private thoughts, I scream in agony. She can see it all. Every single moment I've spent with Adelasia and every conflicting emotion that came with them.

Most importantly though, Amatisi sees that I have no intentions of killing Adelasia, because her heart was always destined to belong to me.

Amatisi lets me go and begins to laugh uncontrollably.

"Oh, what a beautiful circumstance be this!" she purrs before turning to face her sisters. "Our noble King of the Damned has gone and fallen in love with the human sacrifice!"

The rest of the Priestesses and Dravon begin snickering. Amatisi turns her attention to me once more, gripping me with her long nails by the jaw. "Your wayward heart is the reason you're in this situation in the first place, but I am done giving you time to fix your mistake."

Amatisi lets me go, and then from the ground, plumes of black fog begin to rise. My heart sinks and I'm suddenly filled with the worst kind of dread imaginable.

"No!" I growl.

From the fog, three of the most wretched abominations the Priestesses have ever created rise. *Griefclaws.* They stand even taller than I, their limbs unnaturally proportioned, with claws protruding from their fingertips that are so long they scrape across the ground when they move. Their eyes are nothing but depthless voids and their mouths are nothing but rows and rows of sharp teeth and the rotting remnants of the flesh of their last meals. Their skin is brownish gray and stretched tightly across their bony frames.

They make unnerving chittering noises as they await instructions. They are the Priestesses' most loyal, unquestioning servants, designed only to bring grief as their names suggest. They are lethal. So dangerous that even I know better than to foolishly say I'm not afraid of them.

Amatisi approaches her pets and strokes their chests as if in comfort. "Bring her to me, my children. Alive."

Eighteen
Adelasia

    The air in the room has gone icy cold. So has my blood.

    A monster standing even taller than Kaius lingers down the hall from where Saddiq and I cower. Unnaturally long limbs add to its unsettling appearance, and it stands in a cloud of its own foul, festering stink of rotting flesh. Claws hang from its fingertips down to the ground, scraping lightly as it slowly pads down the stone hall. It's not coming directly for me though, it's staring straight ahead.

I quietly and slowly move my legs and the bottom of my dress away from its path as it inspects the space just inches from me.

My heart sinks even further into the floor when another one crawls toward us, its spine contorted awkwardly on the ceiling. The creatures chitter gutturally to each other.

They're communicating, but they're paying no attention to me or Saddiq.

Saddiq takes a loose stone from his cell and tosses it away from us through the iron bars. The creatures lunge for the stone and begin ripping at the empty space with their deadly claws.

Of course. He was a demon hunter. He's trying to show me that the creatures are blind. They can't see us, but they can hear us, and Saddiq tossing that stone might have saved my life. He has some semblance of protection in his cell, but I am fully exposed in this narrow corridor.

As the creatures flail their deadly limbs around the space looking for something that is not there, one of them snuffs out the only lit torch on the wall, leaving us in complete darkness.

I squeeze Saddiq's hand, and though I don't want to, I know that I *have to* leave him if I want to live. I let him go and crawl along the dirty ground, shaking and silently crying.

I hear the monster's claws scraping against stone and screeching. Saddiq must have thrown another rock to help me.

I can't see anything, and my heart is pounding so hard in my ears that I fear I wouldn't be able to hear those creatures even if they were right next to me.

Thankfully, I've visited Saddiq enough times that I can remember the general direction I need to go to lead me out of the dungeon. My fingertips brush along the doorway of the tunnel, and I sit up on my knees and feel for the handle. It creaks as I open it, and I whimper when I hear the creatures screech at the sound. They're coming. I have to run. I stand and push through the doorway, closing it behind me as they crash against the metal. I use every bit of my strength to shut the door, but they are too strong.

I can hear Saddiq yelling, trying to get their attention, but I'm screaming now too.

Screaming for *Kaius*.

The longer I'm trapped against this door, the more frantic I'm becoming. To my right, a torch sits, barely still alight. I pull it off the wall and shove it into the face of one of the creatures. It screeches in pain and falls backward, allowing me just enough of a break in its strength to close and lock the door.

I can hear them beating at the wood, trying to get to me, and though I'm once again in the dark, I let out the shakiest breath of relief at the sense of safety I have with the barrier between me and those things.

I take a big step to the side to brace my back against the wall for stability. My legs are wobbly and I'm lightheaded from screaming for so long. I let my head fall back against the wall as I refill my lungs.

Then I hear another monster chittering.

This time, directly above my head.

My heart is in my feet at this point, and the other two monsters in the dungeons are now beating against the heavy door again. The one above my head lets out a guttural moan as it waits for the others to break out.

I have no choice. I have to run. I try to swallow, but I can't. I try to breathe, but I can't. My body is shaking as my survival instincts attempt to form an escape plan.

The creatures finally break through the door and all I can do is run.

I don't know how or why, but there is something within me guiding my path. An intuition of sorts, and I can only hope it's bringing me to Kaius.

I finally exit the tunnels and head straight for the main corridor of the palace. I can hear more of those things chasing me. My heart races dangerously fast at the possibility of them catching me. Panic engulfs my senses—making it hard to breathe or see or think.

All I want is Kaius.

The throne room. I can see the heavy door now. A small semblance of hope rushes through me, but I feel a tug on the skirt of my dress and stumble to the floor. One of the creatures has dug its claws into the small train of my skirt. Its razor-sharp claws rip the fabric to shreds, allowing an easy but very close escape.

I burst through the throne room door. Fearful tears rush down my face and my eyes meet Kaius'. I stumble to the ground in front of him. My mind is racing with confusion to see him chained and gagged with shadows, wrestling against his restraints to break free.

Dravon is sitting on Kaius' throne, and behind me, there are nine figures in deep gray robes that cover them from head to toe. Those monsters that were chasing me through the palace are kept outside of the throne room by some kind of magic ward. They can't break through this one no matter how hard they claw at it and slam into it with their bodies.

One of the robed figures steps towards me, and I scoot away from them from my place on the floor. The figure tilts its head slightly, and then a grumbly feminine voice emerges from under the veil.

"My dear, you have nothing to fear from me," she whispers.

"Who are you?" I demand.

"My name is Amatisi. I am Matriarch of the Coven of the Ten Priestesses." She gestures behind her to the other figures. "These are my sisters. Zecate. Gaia. Octavia. Marcella. Nephele. Selene. Viseria. Nyx. We hail from the Blackwood, and have come to collect on a thousand-year-old debt owed to us by Kaius Voroninov, King of Bloodlust, Betrayal and the Damned."

Suddenly, an invisible force moves me to my feet, causing me to gasp. Amatisi grabs me gently by the jaw, tilting my head from side to side while my limbs are held down against my will. She lets me go, but I'm still frozen in place as she circles me, toying with my hair–pinching and poking at my body as my dancing masters used to.

"What is your name, love?"

I don't answer her, my mind still in survival mode. I'm not sure I even *remember* my name.

She hits me as Dravon did when I didn't give him the answer he wanted. I taste blood on my tongue and spit it to the side.

"Adelasia," I whisper, and then she sets me on my feet.

"*Pleasure*," Amatisi retorts with venom. "Well, sweet Adelasia, I have a story to tell you about my sister Yekaterina."

I lift my chin slightly. "Kaius already told me about her–about what she did to him and his mother before he killed her. About how you cursed him for it."

"Ah! Well then, I suppose it should come as no surprise to you that we're here, then. How brave you are for facing the prospect of your death by warming your murderer's bed."

I give Kaius a hateful glare. "I would never warm his bed," I say to her, while keeping my eyes on him. He can't answer me, gagged by some dark magic. His eyes fill with despair, though I can't help but see it as some insincere trick.

Amatisi begins laughing. A tear slips down my cheek as I look at the man I've learned to trust over these weeks. A man that I allowed myself to be vulnerable with. A man I've kissed and come to care about.

Kaius watches the tear fall down my cheek. The furrow of his brow reveals the same devastation I feel.

My hand trembles as I reach around the back of my neck, my fingers trailing the top of the raised scar that ends there.

All this time, I really have been a prisoner, and I've finally come to the day of my execution.

With the weight of the truth on my shoulders, Amatisi approaches me from behind and shoves me to the ground. My knees hit the floor with a loud crack, and Amatisi uses her sharp fingernails to rip the back of my dress to shreds, revealing the damning scar along my spine. I sob as I hold one arm up around my chest to keep myself modest and place the other against the cold floor to hold myself upright. Amatisi runs her finger along my spine, and bile rises in my throat at the sensation.

A teardrop lands on my forearm, and I watch it trail down to the floor, leaving a wet streak on its way down, glimmering slightly against the magic marking on my wrist.

I notice it seems to be...alive. It moves as if more magic is flowing through my veins than ever before.

With the utmost subtlety, I look at Kaius from under my wet lashes. I meet his gaze, then look to my wrist before looking back to him. He nods back with a simple tilt of his head.

He's given me his magic. He's trying to help me.

Still looking at the ground, I ask aloud, "Does he have to be the one to do it?"

Amatisi lifts my chin, using her thumb to wipe away one of my tears. "My dear sister has been lost for a thousand years. How poetic it is that you have her beauty."

Amatisi opens her palm, and a dagger conjures into her hand. I recognize it well. Silver blade, ruby pommel. It's the dagger Kaius carries with him everywhere.

She runs the blade roughly along my cheek. It stings, but when I touch my skin, expecting the warmth of my blood, there's nothing. My eyes meet her veiled head, confusion etched in the furrow of my brow.

"The blade remains blunt until wielded by the cursebreaker."

"Enough of these theatrics!" Dravon shouts, grabbing me by the hair and pulling me to my feet. The tip of his blade digs into the side of my throat.

Kaius remains bound and helpless, but Amatisi holds up her arms in surrender at the threat on my life.

I may be just a human, but her sister's soul resides within mine, and that makes me valuable.

Losing me *scares* her.

I whimper softly when Dravon increases the pressure of his blade on my neck. I feel blood begin to trickle down my throat and soak into the collar of my shredded dress.

"You said I would rule over the vampires!"

"When Kaius is *mortal* again, you fool! Release the sacrifice, or witness my fury."

Dravon growls against my ear. "Give me your word."

Amatisi immediately relaxes her shoulders and holds out her hand to him. An offer to make a vow. Dravon pushes me away. I crawl to Kaius, shielding myself behind his frame. Whatever magic was holding him hostage dissipates, and he forces me to stand with him, still using his body to protect me as he digs the stake out of his stomach.

I watch as Dravon takes Amatisi's hand. The moment he does, the skin of his fingers turns a sickly gray color. It begins to trail up his arm, melting away his clothing.

Dravon stumbles backward, clutching his arm to his chest. "What have you done to me?! Witch!"

Dravon begins wailing in pain, falling to the ground as his body convulses and contorts unnaturally. His hair falls off, his teeth grow sharper, his eyes recede into his skull until they're depthless black voids.

When he stops fighting, he rises to his feet as a Griefclaw.

Amatisi hisses and waves her hand towards the door. Dravon—or the creature that has taken over Dravon's body—races towards its siblings at the door and waits outside of it as the others are.

"He's too impulsive to lead, and he could not be controlled."

Kaius scoffs. "Is that what your coven is truly after? Control? You've corrupted your purpose."

"*You* corrupted our purpose!" Amatisi shouts, her demonic voice booming. "You stole away my sister."

"Yekaterina was the worst of you."

"And yet you fell in love with her like a fool! Do not blame your wayward heart on her. You knew exactly who she was."

"You're right. I was a fool. And I've been punished for a thousand years because of it!"

Amatisi shoves the silver dagger into Kaius' grip. "Then break the curse. Your freedom awaits."

His throat bobs with uneasy slowness as he turns to look at me. His eyes, vulnerable and sorrowful, gaze into my soul as he steps closer. With his back to Amatisi, she cannot see what I can—his fear. The slight furrow in his brow gives away his intentions. The magical marking on my wrist burns and tingles. He is silently begging me to save myself in whatever form I can. He doesn't want this to be the end for me, even if it was meant to be.

Amatisi rubs my shoulders, attempting to comfort me while she holds me still from behind, making sure I don't run when Kaius strikes.

A choked gasp leaves my throat as his fingers tighten around the dagger in his hand and his arms tense— ready to end me and take what he's always wanted.

Before I fully close my eyes and brace for the inevitable, I notice the gem around Kaius' neck radiating a dark energy. It knows my life is ending, and it reaches for its master trapped within my soul.

"Eternity forgive me," Kaius whispers as he leans forward and tenderly kisses my forehead. Amatisi snickers behind me, and I whimper when Kaius raises the dagger. I tighten my eyes shut and hold my breath.

I cry out when I feel a pressure in my chest, but it's unlike anything I was expecting. It's not painful at all.

Perhaps it's the knowledge that death will arrive anyway that makes me curious, but I peek and look down, only to find that Kaius' forearm and hand have gone straight through my chest. Not as he did when he ripped out the hearts of his servants, but as if I'm made of some sort of otherworldly presence. A mist. An illusion.

The marking on my wrist glimmers triumphantly. I don't know how I've managed to save myself, but Kaius doesn't dwell on it the way I do. I feel his arm tense, and when he pulls it free from my body, Amatisi's Bloodstone necklace is in his fist. In an instant, the blood rushes to his eyes, forcing them to go black. Some sort of ward wraps around me like a cocoon of safety, and Kaius lets out a roar of fury as he uses both of the Bloodstones in his possession to conjure a red orb of magic.

Amatisi raises her hands to fend off Kaius' spells, but she's no match for the power of two Bloodstones. Kaius rips the second stone from his neck, holding one in each fist. Then, he slams his hands into the marble floor, causing it to crack under his fury. In a flurry of black ashes, Amatisi, the other Priestesses, and the Griefclaws vanish, leaving behind only gray smoke where they once stood.

The ward surrounding me fades. Kaius' eyes return to their normal crimson hue, and he gives me a hollow look–a troubling one–before his eyes roll back into his head and he collapses to the floor.

I lunge for him to try and catch him, barely managing to cup the back of his head.

He feels even colder than usual.

His face and neck are covered in blackish veins that pulsate with an eerie, unsettling red glow. The magic of two Bloodstones must be far out of his capability to wield safely.

I open his tunic to find the markings tracing down, following every vein within him. The damage is deep and far beyond anything I could possibly help with.

I gently rest his head on my lap and try to use what little magic he granted to me to help him heal faster, but it only seems to make the aura emanating from him more volatile.

In a desperate attempt to defy the Priestesses and protect me, he might have suffered irreparable damage, leaving him drained, vulnerable, and weak. I look around desperately. The Priestesses are gone, but I know Amatisi could return at any moment, and she won't hesitate to finish what they started. I can't let that happen.

"Kaius?" I whisper. No response.

It's unnerving, the way the immortals are unnaturally still. He does not have to breathe as I do, but to see him appear truly lifeless and inhuman for the first time is an uncomfortable revelation.

There is nothing I can do for him. He made his choice, and while I can thank him for sparing me, I have an opportunity here to reclaim my life. To return home.

I cannot let the pain in my heart outweigh my good sense.

So I gently rest Kaius' head on the marble floor, and take control of my fate once again.

Nineteen
Adelasia

With limited time to escape, I work quickly. I gather a spare change of clothes and most importantly, stop in the kitchen for food and a water satchel. The vampire servants have all fallen into a still sleep as Kaius has, leaving the palace empty of all life.

After I gather about a week's worth of provisions, I run as quickly as I can to the prisons. Saddiq is hunched over in his cell, some blood dripping from a shallow claw mark in his stomach.

He looks shocked to see me, but I don't have time to explain right now. With Dravon gone, the magic holding Saddiq in his cell has collapsed, allowing me to freely pass through the doorway. I kneel in front of my friend and hold out some bread and cheese for his angry stomach. He whimpers as the small amount of food slivers down his parched throat. I hold the water satchel to his mouth for him to sip.

"You're alive!"

"Shhh," I coo with urgency. "Can you stand? We need to leave. Now."

"Adelasia—"

"I'll explain later. Please, *please* stand up."

I use my strength to lift him to his feet. Once he steadies himself, I hand him another small piece of bread and a cleaver I stole from the kitchen.

We wordlessly escape the prison and without looking back, we run from the valley as quickly as Saddiq's weak legs will carry him.

When his energy depletes just as we lose sight of the edge of the forest, it begins to rain. Saddiq and I take shelter under the roots of a large tree, sharing a single cloak and our body heat for warmth. Neither of us are brave enough to start a fire. The Blackwood is already a dangerous place for two humans. The unnecessary attention a fire would bring would only lessen our already abysmal odds of making it out of this forest alive.

Since I've become accustomed to the night, I allow him to rest on my shoulder while I keep watch.

Our survival is only attributed to the rain masking our scents. When the dawn comes, I wake up Saddiq and share a slice of bread with him. We have no way of knowing how deep into the forest we are, and neither of us are in a condition to hunt. Plants in the Blackwood are not edible, and water sources are scarce and guarded by beasts and demons.

Saddiq is clearly feeling stronger, and as we make our way through the forest, he leads us. Every branch snapping or insect buzzing heightens our anxiety, until it gets so bad that the sounds of our own breathing make us jump.

"Will you tell me what happened?" Saddiq asks.

I've been avoiding this topic since we escaped; not because I have anything to hide, but because there is a large part of my heart that still aches when I think about Kaius. I thought I could trust him, and I thought that perhaps he saw something special between us. Something more than just...fate.

Every stolen glance, every caress of his lips, and every tender graze of his fingers were only a means to an end. I was a pawn in a game I didn't even know we were playing.

What a fool I was.

I swallow, the action burning my sore, parched throat. "I didn't listen to you," I admit. "About trusting the vampires. About...trusting Kaius."

Tears gather in my eyes on their own accord but I blink them away, my voice quivering. "He was going to kill me all along."

Saddiq comes to a stop and pulls me in for a gentle hug. He's still so skinny. Hugging him back feels like I might break him in half. We are dirty and stale, but I let him hold me as I hug him back.

"Why did you come for me in the prisons? The ward was broken. I could have found my own way out."

"Because you deserve a chance at freedom too, and I thought we'd have better odds together."

Saddiq pulls away and smiles gently. "You're right about that. Look." He gestures to a group of rocks behind me. They're painted with fading runes I don't recognize.

"When I was a demon hunter before I was captured, my men and I would leave these runes around the forest to remember which beasts lived in the area." He brings us closer to the rocks. "I recognize these stones." He looks up and around, then points to a darker part of the forest just ahead. "The edge of the forest is a two-day trip that way. There's a spring of freshwater about ten miles from here. We should reach it before the next night falls. We have a small burrow covered by thick leaves and debris in the area—we would be safe there until morning, maybe even catch some game."

I nod and then gesture in the direction of some bushes. Saddiq understands, and quietly turns his back to give me some privacy. I take a moment to relieve myself behind the foliage and then emerge.

When I come back out into the open, Saddiq and I both hear a branch snap in the distance. He and I take shelter behind trees at opposite ends of the clearing.

From the direction we just came from, a pack of three werewolves emerge from the trees. They sniff the ground, each inhale bringing them closer and closer to us.

Saddiq slowly and silently bends down to pick up a rock, throwing it as far as he can away from both of us. The werewolves disappear back into the trees in the direction of the rock. Saddiq and I make eye contact and sigh in relief, but something catches his eyes behind me, and he goes pale. I shakily turn my head, but a large, wet snout touches the base of my neck. Drool drips down my collarbone when the werewolf licks my skin.

A cold shiver snakes down my body at the feeling. The beast growls. I whimper. Saddiq looks horrified. He has a chance to escape while they're preoccupied with me. The smell of Kaius–of vampire–likely still lingers on my filthy skin. The other three werewolves return, surrounding me as they take turns sniffing and nipping at my ankles.

They're taunting me. They want me to run so they can get the thrill of the hunt before killing me.

I give a sorrowful goodbye look to my friend before I jump and roll through the space between two of the wolves. I don't look back as I run to the opposite end of the clearing, as far away from Saddiq as I can go. The wolves growl as they chase me. I reach a tree and begin climbing as fast as I can. My fingertips are bloody from digging so hard into the bark. Only three steps up the trunk, I lose my footing and slip. My back lands on the dirt and the wind exits my lungs from the impact.

I roll to my left just as a set of razor-sharp claws slice into the space where I was just lying, leaving three jagged lines in the dirt.

I push myself up, forcing my body to move despite the pain. I look to Saddiq, equally as desperate as I am for safety. He swings his cleaver with skill, but the wolves are so fast.

I lunge for him, hoping to offer him some help, but a wolf leaps into me, sending me flying in the opposite direction and knocking me into a tree.

When I fall back to the ground, my temple connects with the jagged edge of a rock, and I feel warmth rush down my face as I try to sit up, only to fall to the side once again. The world starts spinning, and everything starts fading to black.

I hear Saddiq yelling my name, but he seems so distant now. His voice fades in and out with the snarling of the wolves.

I watch a wolf raise its hackles at a silhouette in the distance, surrounded by a soft silver aura.

So pretty, I think to myself, before an unimaginable pain cuts through my stomach, and I let the darkness take me.

When I wake, the ground is cool.

No. Not the ground. My fingers. My body. I'm so cold. Cold and weak.

I open my eyes to find raindrops caught in my lashes and my clothing soaked through. My head aches as I lift it slightly. My neck feels far too heavy and lands back down with a *crack* on a rock below me.

"Saddiq?" I croak, unable to bring my voice above a loud whisper. My mind races as I try to remember the moments before everything went dark.

I remember Saddiq begging me to get up and run. I remember him screaming when one of the werewolves ripped his arm clean off his body. I remember blood. So much blood. His. Mine. The wolves'.

My body shudders with a sob as I look around the clearing only to see three dead wolves. No fourth wolf. No Saddiq.

He's gone. My only friend from my captive life has been killed because I dragged him into this forest with me.

He died trying to save me when he had every opportunity to run.

While my sobs grow louder, my fear keeps them partially suppressed. Now I'm alone in this forest, lost and injured with the guilt of costing my friend his life weighing down on my shoulders.

I sniffle and use a tree trunk for balance as I stand. The claw marks on the side of my stomach burn unnaturally. I look down and move the tattered remains of my top to the side to find the injury oozing blood and a sticky black substance that smells foul.

I notice then, among the black ooze and my crimson blood, that packed into my wound there are small flower blossoms. I recognize them instantly—*Witchfoil*—used to temporarily stave off the adverse effects of supernatural injuries. It's not a cure for the toxins that coat a werewolf's claws, but it's usually mixed with a sedative to ease the passing of one who has been injured. The plant isn't rare, but it requires entering the Blackwood to find it. Most aren't brave enough to do so themselves, and what stock human apothecaries have is exceedingly expensive, and so those of us who are unfortunate enough to find ourselves at the mercy of a werewolf scratch die an agonizingly painful death within hours.

I stumble across the clearing as the world spins and my body aches. I don't even know where I'm going, but I do not want to die here alone in the Blackwood Forest, and so I walk, hoping to find some end-of-life comforts in the soft trickle of a freshwater spring, or even the familiar beauty of a blooming rose. My brain throbs and my blood pounds in my ears with every step until finally–*finally*–I reach a wide river.

My parched throat burns as I fall to my knees and lean over to sip the freshwater. I sigh with relief at the feeling of the cool drink making its way down my throat. I use one of my hands to scoop the water into my mouth, unable to quench my thirst fast enough. As my hand reaches into the water for the third time, a thick vine shoots out from under the water, wraps around my waist, and pulls me under. The water then shifts from crystal clear to pitch black.

An illusion. A trap.

I begin panicking as the vines pull me further under the water. I can't see or feel anything except the vines squeezing me painfully and the water running through my hair as I get pulled deeper and deeper into the river. I scream. I kick. I thrash. All of it is to no avail and my panic has stolen what precious breath I had left in my lungs.

I begin to convulse as my body searches for air that isn't there–and suddenly, I feel lighter. As the weight of the water crushes down on my breathless chest, I no longer feel fear or pain. I no longer feel anger towards Kaius and I no longer miss my mother.

As I begin to drift into that eternal sleep...I feel the peaceful abyss of nothing.

Twenty
Kaius

Please, please, please, I beg of you—let me in. Show me where you are.

My only solace to be found as I search for Adelasia deep in the Blackwood is that I can still feel my magic tethered to her. While it cannot guide me, it's proof that she's still alive.

To know that she was so angry with me and felt so betrayed by my lies that she would risk her life in the most dangerous territory in the world only goes to show how fractured her heart is. I cannot bear the thought of her dying, let alone dying because of me.

I can't imagine she got very far, but in the time I was recovering from the dark magic's effects on my body, she could have gone any number of ways. She could be anywhere, and my mind only races with terrible assumptions.

The forest air is so thick with foul magic that it makes her scent nearly impossible to pick up. She could be bleeding out ten feet from me and I wouldn't know. All I have to rely on is my sight and sound.

I find myself in a clearing and before me lie three werewolf carcasses. I rush to them to find them surrounding a pool of dried blood. I grab a handful of the dirt and the blood to inhale deeply, half-relieved and half-afraid when I catch the sweet scent of Adelasia, nearly fully engulfed by the smell of her terror.

I examine the werewolves to find deep lacerations in their torsos. Werewolf skin is too thick for a human's blade to penetrate this deep. Whatever killed these creatures had supernatural strength.

That in turn means that whatever killed these creatures probably has Adelasia, too.

And then it happens.

I feel the icy-cold spear of dread rip through my very soul as all of my magic comes rushing back to me in an instant. I can do nothing but fall to my knees, gasping for air that I do not need; clutching my chest to feel a heart that does not beat.

"No," I whisper to myself.

It's not true. It can't be. This is some vile trick of the forest. *She's not dead. She can't be.*

The weight of the pain in my chest makes it hard to stand, but I force myself to my feet and cry out her name over and over, searching for any sign of her at all.

I pause when I hear something in the distance. A gagging sort of sound like when humans are sick. And then a labored inhale, and a wet cough.

It must be her. It has to be. I close my eyes and will all of my focus into tracking which direction she's in. On the wind, I catch the smell of stale water…infected flesh…*lavender.*

I sprint through the forest towards the smell, and only through the grace of my supernatural sight do I spot her in the distance, face down on the bank of a river.

"Adelasia!"

I rush over to her, only to find myself still filled with dread as I gently flip her over and take her in. Her eyes are sunken and dark. Blood pools in her tear ducts and drips out of her nose. Her skin has gone gray and the claw marks at her side ooze far too much blood for her to make it much longer. She's soaked through to the bone and shivering.

I need to get her back to the Obsidian Palace. Now.

I pick her up and hold her tight to my chest as I sprint faster than my supernatural speed has ever carried me. Adelasia moans in pain, coughing out blood and the toxins invading her body.

When I make it back to the valley, I immediately bring her to my bed. I force her to drink a tonic for the pain, and then begin cleaning her wound.

As I scrape out the hardened toxins from the gashes, I find Witchfoil tightly and skillfully packed into it. No human in her condition could have done this on their own. *First the wolves...now the blossoms...*

I know the tonic has done its job when I rub a thick cream over the wound and she doesn't scream, and the temporary paralytic properties keep her still.

I am no medicinal expert, but I've seen my fair share of werewolf injuries over my lifetimes to know how to treat them.

But I've never had to do so on a human, and deep within me, I know there's no guarantee that she will survive. It terrifies me.

After I clean her wound and cover it with the highly concentrated Witchfoil salve, I hover my hands over the injury and close my eyes.

I concentrate on healing magic, willing the Bloodstone around my neck to help her.

In response, I feel nothing. Not even a whisper of magic. I open my eyes and stare at my hands before trying again. I watch as a faint glow radiates from my fingers and then dissipates before reaching Adelasia.

My mouth falls open in desperation and confusion. I don't understand. I remove the chain of the Bloodstone from my neck and stare at it. It has completely lost its aura—as if I stole too much magic when I used Amatisi's stone with Yekaterina's to banish the Priestesses.

Adelasia's wound suddenly begins to fade to grey and then black. The salve is failing. She will die.

"No," I whisper to myself. I don't know what to do. I've always relied on my magic in dire situations. I don't know how to help her.

I press my palms to my eyes, trying to think of what to do—and then it occurs to me that there may only be one option.

Quickly, I conjure a knife in my hand and slice open my palm. On the floor of my room, I use my blood to vaguely create the shape of an eight-pointed star. In the center, I place both of the Bloodstones, and then I kneel and place my forehead to the cold marble floor.

I recite an ancient language that's long been forgotten. The air in the room seems to shift, and I feel an evil presence standing over me.

I raise my head slightly, but a force keeps it down.

A husky female voice that rumbles through my bones snarls at me.

"I have not permitted you to look upon me," it says. My desperate pleas that I have lined up in my throat die there, and I wait for permission to speak.

Before me, I have summoned *the one*.

Eternity. Goddess of Magic and Misery.

"It has been a long time since I have been summoned to this plane," she says. I keep my eyes downward and my lips tight. "There are few who know how to do so. Even fewer are foolish enough to try." She pauses for a moment, and subtly I raise my eyes to just barely catch the Goddess looking to Adelasia. I cannot make out her face or any of her features. I can only see the glimmering black robe she wears, identical to the ones the Priestesses wear.

"You wish to bargain," she finally says, and then she walks to Adelasia's bedside. With Eternity's back turned, I lift my head to watch her stroke Adelasia's cheek. Then she lowers her veil over her head and turns to me. "She is destined for the grave."

"Can you save her?" I ask quietly.

Eternity snickers and then approaches me. She stands at about Adelasia's height, the eight-pointed crown of black crystals sitting heavy atop her head, reaching upward like claws.

"Perhaps," she whispers. "But tell me, Kaius Voroninov, is that truly what you want?"

Her voice enters my ear in a sensual way, and then she summons a mirror in front of us. In the reflection, I see an apparition of Adelasia standing next to Eternity, my body nowhere to be found.

"I think in your heart lies another desire," she hisses. "After all these years of waiting, don't you wonder what that looks like?" Adelasia's ghost fades from the mirror, and in her place—a man.

He has dark hair and bright green eyes—a familiar and handsome smirk on his lips.

It's not until Eternity raises a hand and strokes my cheek with her fingers and I watch as she does the same thing in the mirror that I realize who this man is.

Me.

Or at least who I used to be, a thousand years ago.

I open my mouth and find no fangs in my reflection, and before I get a chance to close my mouth, the reflection morphs into me again—only this time in the present.

And for the first time, I'm allowed to see truly what a monster I have become. My red eyes are not inviting. My white hair stands out harshly from my skin. The handsome smirk I had previously has been washed away by a permanent frown and an unmovable furrow in my brow.

I close my eyes and turn my head away from the mirror. Eternity laughs into my ear, mocking my disdain for myself.

"I've been watching you for a long time, Son of Crows. How fragile you are to give up one desire for another so easily. I can save the girl...but what is it you will offer me in return?"

"Anything," I answer absolutely. "You can have anything you want...just don't take her from me. Please."

"*Anything?*" she repeats curiously. "Have some dignity; I do not find pleasure in watching you beg. How much is her human soul worth to you?"

"Everything."

"A soul for a soul, then?" she offers. "One of my choosing."

"You can have a thousand souls if you wish. Just not hers."

"Careful," she warns, "Desperation is not a bargaining tool."

"She is the only soul that I care for."

Eternity hums as if she doesn't believe me, but she holds out her hand to me. I take it. Dark magic on our skin forms a crimson line.

A blood vow with the Goddess of Misery; one that will not be broken.

When she releases my hand, she uses her magic to lift the two Bloodstones at eye level. Her dark magic surrounds them, crushing them together until they form a single stone just a smidge larger than their original size.

She plucks it from the space in front of her and hands it to me.

"You only delay the inevitable," she says as I take it and place it around my neck. I approach Adelasia and focus on healing her wound. "I have seen millions of futures. Infinite forevers. There are none where your mate does not perish."

I swallow cautiously, keeping my focus on Adelasia. When I once again feel the soft warmth radiating from her body, only then do I turn to face the dark Goddess.

But she has vanished, leaving me wondering who I have just sacrificed for this sinister pact.

Though some of the radiant flush of Adelasia's cheeks has returned, I still fear that I was too late–that by some twisted version of fate, I've only prolonged her suffering instead of saving her.

Eternity did not specify when Adelasia would die, just that she would spare her this once. But for how long? A day? A week? A century?

I lift my hand to Adelasia's supple cheek and stroke her soft skin with the back of my fingers.

I watch as her arm reveals goosebumps at my lifeless, cold touch. I retract my hand and feel a sense of dread and guilt for ever bringing her here. I stole her from her life, only to cause her harm and misery.

"It's like you were created solely to be my ruin, my sweet agony", I whisper across her lips, barely grazing them with mine as I place the most featherlight of kisses there. "But we both know you were meant for more than that, don't we?"

I take a deep, defeated breath, and my voice shakes as I tell her still body, "Everyone dies. And one day in the future, when it's your time, your memories of me will die with you. But for me? I'll carry you with me for the rest of my miserable eternity."

Twenty-One
Adelasia

Somehow, in the vast expanse of nothing, I feel a hand reaching for mine. A warm hand. It grips my slender, freezing fingers and I feel it pull me in the opposite direction of the vines around my ankles.

The pulling becomes more frantic, more painful, until finally–*light*.

I see light. And in that light, I can make out the shape of a person. A man.

When I crash through the surface back into the air, my lungs ache for it. I wretch to clear them of water and replace it with deep breaths.

I feel the man that pulled me out of the water rub circles on my back and hold my loose hair out of the way of my gagging as a black, tar-like substance escapes my throat.

I turn my head to face the man, and through the thick haze of the poison in my body that clouds my vision and thoughts, I see wings.

Large, beautiful, white wings, surrounding us in a protective embrace. My shaky hand reaches for the feathers as if they will bring me comfort...but then he's gone.

"Kaius?" I croak. And then he's there again.

The feathers...no...his cloak.

But his cloak is black, not white, right?

I can't see.

I can't feel.

I can't remember.

I jolt upright in a fright to the sound of thunder, only to find the room empty. I'm in the Obsidian Palace, under warm covers in a fireplace-lit comfort. My robe is thrown over my vanity chair, and I stand to put it on over my thin nightgown to protect myself from the chill in the air I've only just begun to become accustomed to.

My abdomen burns when I move, and after I slip my robe over my shoulders, I lift the hem of my nightgown to find that the werewolf's deep claw marks have faded into a thin layer of healing pink skin. There is little evidence of the grueling injury that may be fading on the surface–but is forever burned into my memory.

To know that such pain and suffering preceded the slow deaths of my father and brother makes my stomach ill. I swallow the bile creeping up my throat and leave my room. My body aches as I walk, so I have to slow down my pace to ease the discomfort. It does little to help.

I feel weak and feverish, hot and cold. Waves of nausea and headaches pass through my system one after another, giving me no reprieve.

Finally, I see him.

He's on the balcony, hunched over the thick stone railing, standing in the pouring rain. Lightning dances across the sky and thunder booms over the palace, shaking the floor under my bare feet. It must keep him from hearing me.

When I step onto the balcony myself, the cold rain instantly soaks me to the bone, making my aches worse and my shivers nearly unbearable. I reach for him, resting my hand gently on his shoulder. He spins, clutching my wrist tightly in his as he faces me, looking as if I've genuinely startled him.

"Adelasia," he breathes, almost with relief in his voice, though his face shows concern. "What are you doing out here? You should be resting. You–"

His train of thought is interrupted by me throwing myself into his arms. I begin to sob into his chest. He doesn't embrace me back, but he allows me to hold him in the dense rain. "You came for me..." I whisper into his neck, so afraid that this is a dream and I'm still in the forest. Still cold and alone and an inch from death.

Finally, he wraps his arms around me, matching my embrace. He very gently lifts me and carries me through the doorway, shielding us from the rain. He holds me against the cold wall of the hallway so I no longer have to stand on my weak legs.

"Of course I did," he breathily whispers as he presses our foreheads together. "If there was ever a moment where you doubted that, then I must spend the rest of my days restoring your faith in me."

The strands of hair that frame his face drip cold water onto his cheeks, and I brush the hair away so I can see him in all his vampiric, splendid beauty.

"I'm sorry I ran," I whisper in shame.

His shoulders seem to melt away centuries of tension at my apology. "Please never do it again. I've lived for over a thousand years and nothing has ever terrified me more than the state I found you in."

"How did you know I was in the river?"

He doesn't answer me, but I watch his jaw tighten at my question as if he's trying to find the answer himself. But then, he gently presses his lips to mine. The pain melts away, as does the fear and my conflicting feelings for him.

He gently breaks the kiss, because we both know there are fractures in our story that cannot be fixed with intimacy. I need truth. I need trust.

"Do you still intend to kill me?" I ask softly.

"No," he whispers absolutely. "I made a deal with the Dark Goddess to ensure you would remain breathing. You will not live a short life, Adelasia."

"You...made a deal with *Eternity*? You spoke to a goddess...to spare me?" I ask. He shows me his arm and I gently pull up his sleeve to see the lines of the blood vow interwoven with the black line of a broken promise he once showed me. "What was the deal?"

"A soul for a soul."

"Whose soul?"

He uses his hand to cup the back of my head, holding me up with the other. His lips ghost against mine. "So long as it's not yours, I do not care."

I swallow. Is there really no one else he cares for that he would make such a deal to save me? "What about Amatisi? You would defy her and remain cursed for me? Why?"

Kaius' face suddenly hardens into a stoicism I haven't seen in weeks. But within that mask, I see vulnerability, too.

"You know why, my sweet agony. Do not pretend otherwise. She will come for you. For us. She will use her wicked magic to try and tear us apart. She will torture us with our greatest horrors and drown us in the fear of being apart. But she will never take you from me. Do you understand?"

"But what if—"

"Shhh." He quiets me with a soft kiss on my cheek. "Do you understand?"

I nod my head, and Kaius has to hold me steady, as I still feel lightheaded and weak standing on my own. One of his arms wraps around my torso, so we are chest-to-chest, and with the other hand, he lifts my hand to his mouth, pressing his lips to my knuckles.

"I have a favor to ask," I start.

"Anything."

Dread fills my heart as I think about Saddiq. "My friend from the dungeons. I took him into the forest with me and I lost him when the wolves attacked—" I take a deep breath as tears begin to spill out of my eyes. I know in my heart that he's gone, but I owe it to him to at least search for his remains. Perhaps give him a burial and mourn him properly. "Would you please go look for him? I know his chances were few, but if I lived, perhaps he did too. It's my fault he was out there in the first place. I don't want him to feel forgotten."

Kaius nods and rests his forehead against mine. "I shall take a search party into the woods to look, but only on the condition that you promise me you will rest while I'm gone. If there is any toxin still lingering in your blood..."

He need not finish. The fear in his voice is enough.

Twenty-Two
Kaius

I did not have the heart to tell Adelasia that I found Saddiq.

Or at least—what the wolves had left of him: a severed arm and far too much blood.

Still, I cannot in good conscience lie to her about looking for him, so after I saw her to bed myself, I gathered some of my servants and forced them to attend a rescue mission that would reveal nothing I don't already know.

Humans and even younger vampires would find these woods unnavigable, but I have lived in the valley nearly my entire immortal life. Memorized every tree and every rock. Every long-forgotten trap laid by the demon hunters and every bone of a small rabbit caught by a wolf; supernatural or otherwise.

It's a simple task to retrace my steps and find the river where I found Adelasia near death. At the time, I was so concerned with her injuries and getting her somewhere safe that I ignored the obvious signs that someone had gotten there before I did.

She had Witchfoil in her wound, but even more obvious—the feathers.

I have not seen those feathers in nearly six centuries, and I hoped to never see them again. The realization that *he* has been lingering near my home—enough to find helping Adelasia a worthwhile cause—makes my blood boil.

To know that he will use this as a debt I will need to repay makes me blind with rage. In that frenzied anger, I punch the oak to my left.

Combined with my strength and the power of my new Eternity-blessed Bloodstone, the oak is ripped from its roots, falling to the forest floor with a loud boom.

I feel a shock to my system. There is no such being on this earth that was meant to wield that kind of magic. It's dark and twisted and dangerous.

I think it is warning me. I ought not to misuse the power I've now twice stolen from the keepers of magic. Doing so again may have deadly consequences.

One of my thralls approaches from a break in the trees, two other men following. They all meet my eyes and shake their heads.

As I suspected, there was nothing of Saddiq left to find.

As I return home, I close my eyes in relief. Her heartbeat is stronger than it was when I left. I can hear it through the walls. I listen for it, always, because I cannot bear to live in silence without it. Her life brings me peace and comfort where I have none.

I left her to rest in my bed and warded the door. As I enter, even through the darkness I can see that she looks less sickly than she did before. I carefully slide into the bed next to her with my back against the headboard.

Somehow, within her dream, she reaches for me, settling down again by resting her cheek on my thigh. I let my finger trace up and down the scar on her back that hasn't been covered by her nightgown.

In all my years of immortality, it never once crossed my mind that there was a possibility that I could care for the person who would free me from this curse.

But my feelings have gone far beyond care. Far beyond fondness. Maybe even far beyond love. The bond we share is more than a millennium in the making, and I believe it was always meant to happen this way.

A love destined for the grave.

It's a devastating realization that all paths of our love result in me losing her, and that is a reality I have yet to make peace with and refuse to accept.

Eternity already told me that there is no future where my mate does not die, but what if I made another bargain? Is there anything I could offer the Dark Goddess that would save Adelasia from a fate inked in blood? A fate she had no part in curating?

The sun crests and falls again before she stirs and wakes. Her dark lashes flutter open to reveal a confused and slightly concerned look. I use a hand to run my knuckle across her jaw.

"The color has returned to your cheeks," I whisper. "How do you feel?"

"Tired." She runs her hand over her stomach where her wound is and does not flinch or wince. At the same time, it grumbles. "I could use something to eat."

I nod, and as quickly as she finishes her sentence, a tray of breakfast appears on my lap for her. She reaches for the fresh berries first, and then the hot tea, and manages to finish the entire plate except for the bread. I assume that's what she survived on for most of her time in the Blackwood, so I don't protest when she leaves it untouched.

Her eyes meet mine for a moment, and then she lowers her head. "You didn't find him," she says quietly, more to herself than to me.

I shake my head. "I'm sorry," I offer, though my apology is no comfort to her. A lone tear falls down her cheek and I wipe it away with my thumb. "The Blackwood is a deadly place. Do not blame yourself for his death. I know he cared for you. I don't think he'd want you to torture yourself with guilt."

She wraps her delicate fingers around my wrist and leans into my hand that's still pressed to her cheek. I run my thumb across her chapped bottom lip.

"He has a family," she says.

I nod. "Perhaps once you've healed we can travel together to inform them."

She looks at me, and I see a small sparkle of hope in her eyes. "You'd come with me to do that?"

"If it would comfort you even a bit, then yes. Maybe...maybe on the way back we could visit your mother."

"Do you mean it?" she asks.

I nod, but I think she feels as though she won't make it that long, and the thought brings her only more sorrow.

She sighs and lets go of my wrist. I let my hands rest in my lap. She lies back down on her side and furrows her brow.

"My head hurts," she breathes.

"It will take a while for you to fully recover. You are...very lucky, Adelasia. More than you realize."

"Would I truly have died if you didn't bargain with Eternity?" she asks.

The thought alone fills me with dread, but I answer truthfully. "Yes. And before you ask, I would not hesitate to make the same bargain again. Nothing she could take from me would ruin me more than losing you."

"Because we're *mates*?"

"Because..." I trail off and bite my cheek. She closes her eyes and the corner of her mouth tilts up in a smirk. "Something amusing?" I ask, somewhat irritated by her reaction.

"Is it really so hard to simply say that you care about me?"

I open my mouth to tell her just that, but I find the words getting caught in my throat. I come to the realization that I've always spoken in circles, or hidden my real meaning, because denial is easier that way. "There is nothing simple about the way I feel about you."

"It's okay," she sleepily whispers. "You'll stop being such a grumpy tyrant and admit it eventually."

"Grumpy tyrant, hm?" I playfully growl as I settle on my side so I can fully face her. We're nose to nose when she opens her eyes. They're distant. She needs to rest now.

I gently brush a strand of hair from her face and then use my thumb to trace soft circles on her temple. "I think you're right," I whisper to her sleeping form. "But maybe I don't want to be a tyrant anymore. Maybe I will take you across the Endless Sea to the land of mortal kings, where there is no magic, no Priestesses, no demons. Somewhere no one will ever find us...and then maybe I'll finally have the courage to love you simply. Perhaps I'll even have the courage to whisper it to you, too."

She sighs in her heavy sleep. I kiss her hairline and stroke her cheek, carefully watching her breathe.

I suddenly sense an unwelcome presence in the palace. Chills climb up my spine and my body tenses over her protectively. The palace remains silent, but I know better than to ignore my intuition. Someone is here.

Carefully, so I don't wake Adelasia, I slip out of the bed and seal her door with a ward before walking through the halls. Though the unwelcome presence lingers, I don't equate it to a threat. Regardless, red magic wraps around my wrists as I prepare for a fight. I am on edge all the time now, worried that Amatisi has come for Adelasia in her weak state.

"Show yourself!" I hiss into the shadows. My voice echoes through the halls.

The only presence that makes itself known is Cassius. He slithers towards me, slowly, and I notice that some of his scales are missing. I kneel down to take a closer look. He has a gash across his body, black and festering like the one Adelasia had.

I run my hands gently over his scales and the magic of the bloodstone heals the wound. "Did you try to fight off those wolves for our precious Adelasia?" He weakly raises his head as he wraps himself around my arm. "Brave little fool," I murmur. "You seem to always come to her aid before I do. Maybe you'd serve better as her guardian than my companion."

At that, Cassius raises his head again with a new energy.

"Oh? You would like that I see." He nudges against my chin. I lean in closer to whisper. "I think she would like that too. Four hundred years with you at my side, and it seems we've both been bewitched by her."

Cassius' forked tongue pokes out. I sigh and give him a small upturn in the corner of my mouth. "We're in agreement then, to do whatever it takes to protect her life with our own?"

Cassius tightens his coil around my arm, and another golden line appears down his back, intertwining with Adelasia's vow.

My own forearm now has an intricate pattern of red, black, and golden vows.

A promise of blood, a broken fate, and an oath of protection.

How many more can I make before one vow breaks another?

After the glimmering of the line dissipates and the golden threads settle into my skin, Cassius lets out a long hiss that sounds suspiciously like a laugh, and then he fades into dust.

What's left in my palm is a single white feather.

My hand trembles as anger surges through my veins like molten-hot liquid. I clutch my fingers around the feather, and when I reopen my palm, it's been reduced to dust by the strength of my grip. The ashes flutter away with an eerie breeze filtering through the hall.

From the open balcony behind me, I hear a pair of boots land on the stone railing, and then a soft thump as they land on the floor of the terrace and enter the marble halls.

"Leave," I warn without turning around. "Whatever you've heard or seen through Cassius, forget it all and I'll let you leave with your life. Otherwise, there will be no feathers left on your wings for you to taunt me with."

He *tsks* behind me, and his smooth voice fills my ears for the first time in centuries. "This is the warm welcome I get for saving your pet?"

"I cannot offer warmth when you are not welcome to begin with."

"She would have died long before you got there if it weren't for me."

"Your actions lack a distinct taste of altruism," I snap back. I then turn to face him, and my eyes land on a figure I recognize all too well, despite my best efforts to forget. "I do not have the patience right now for your games. This is about her life."

"Ah, which you've so graciously given me the humble task of protecting," he pinches my cheek as a brother would do to a sibling. I jerk away from his touch. "I intend to perform my duty to the letter." He pauses, looks at the mix of desperation and anger on my face, and then begins to laugh. "What's the matter, Kaius? Afraid I can do it better than you? I can promise I'll certainly be *on top of things*."

His innuendo is not lost on me, and I roughly grab his arm. "Break this vow. Now," I demand. "*Now*, Rowan."

His expression glosses over with something solemn. "We both know you're the only one here with a history of breaking vows when it's *convenient* for you." He raises the side of his mouth in a sneer that shows his teeth, before coyly transforming it into a smile and removing himself from my grip. "I'd hate to take that talent from you."

I use the power of the enhanced Bloodstone around my neck to shove him backward, leaving him on his back in the doorway of the balcony. Then, as he tries to bring himself to his feet, I use the dark magic to hold him on his knees.

He gives me a sultry smirk. "Usually you're the one on your knees in front of me. How does that power feel?"

"Sublime," I tell him with a tilt of my head and a wicked smile, before using my magic to force his wings closed, and toss him over the balcony.

Twenty-Three
Kaius

It takes a full week for Adelasia to regain her full strength. By the time she heals, word has spread through the valley of her involvement with me, and what it could mean for the vampire race. The Priestesses are not exactly discreet when it comes to someone defying their power and authority. I'm certain it's their doing that the seeds of distaste for me are sprouting in the valley.

While there are many like me who find no pleasure in this immortal life, there are plenty of others who find freedom in it. Those who would kill to keep it. I cannot let that happen.

Protecting Adelasia was a choice before. It's a need now.

I have no way of knowing if Yekaterina intended for the entire vampire race to weigh on one mortal's shoulders. I have my suspicions that she didn't think this far ahead. The creatures and demons the priestesses create are imperfect things, often requiring several...*generations* before they are ghastly enough for the Coven.

I am the demon Yekaterina never got to perfect, and I know that what's left of her soul squirms at the thought of it—for her to know after all these years that her hold on me is not as absolute as she assumed.

Adelasia has permanently moved into my suite for her own safety, with multiple wards defending the rooms she visits most. The human servants are no longer allowed near her as their minds do not possess the fortitude to block out supernatural influence. I would not put it past the Priestesses to use them as assassins or kidnappers.

Adelasia still mourns the loss of her friend. She built him a shrine in the courtyard and spends much of the time she's awake in the sunlight at it. She must be praying—trying to reach him.

I wonder what she says.

Does she bear her guilt? Does she beg for forgiveness?

Even more selfishly...I wonder if she talks about me. What does she share about us in the confidence of her own mind?

On this night, I do not find her lingering at Saddiq's shrine in the dusk. Instead, she's on the balcony of my suite, watching the sun fall behind the horizon. A near mirror image of the way I used to watch the sunrise.

Her robe billows softly in the wind as I approach. I quietly say her name so I don't startle her. The moonlight soaks into her skin and casts an ethereal glow that seems to radiate from within her. In fact, I know it does. She turns her head just enough to acknowledge me with an emotionless smile, then leans forward, lifts up on her toes slightly, and presses a soft kiss to my cheek.

That's all she offers me before turning away, attempting to leave me on the balcony alone.

I catch her wrist. "Adelasia...you've been distant for days. Please talk to me."

She swallows and stares at me as if I've just asked her an unintelligible question. Her eyes flicker to my lips and then back up to my eyes.

"I...I'm scared," she finally admits after a long silence.

"Of Amatisi?" I ask for clarification.

"Yes," she whispers. "I'm afraid she'll come for me—or worse—turn me against you."

My mouth hangs open in disbelief. I couldn't have heard her correctly. I don't have a chance to continue pondering her words, because she speaks again.

Nervously, she asks, "Are curses spells? With spoken word?"

I furrow my brow and take her hand in mine. "Yes."

"What is yours?"

I swallow the protest in my throat. I don't enjoy speaking the words aloud, in fact, I can't remember a time where I have. I've written it enough times that it may as well be etched into my pale skin.

"Blessed be, Eternity,

Ten centuries of enmity.

Mortality evade the soul,

Bloodlust consume him whole.

On scar of skin,

Find mark of sin.

Hilt of gems with dagger sharp,

This curse shall end,

when death kisses heart."

I slowly pull the dagger from its place in my boot and hold it between us.

Adelasia is my freedom. My unbeating heart. My undying soul.

I turn outward to face the edge of the balcony and with every bit of strength in my coiled muscles, I throw it as far as I can. It lands somewhere beyond the valley in the forest.

But just as quickly as it disappears from our vision, a cloud of black dust gathers in my hand, and the dagger appears once more. I can never be rid of it, just as I can never be rid of this curse as long as she stands breathing by my side.

She runs her finger along the sharp blade, gasps, and then holds her hand to her chest. I unfold her fingers to find a small cut on her index finger. I kiss away the single blood drop and then stare at the dagger in a bit of a trance. I lean forward and inhale deeply the scent of her hair so that the taste of her blood does not cloud my thoughts.

"Can I ask you something?" I whisper into the crown of her head. I feel her nod. "When you were in that forest...did you see anyone else? Aside from Saddiq and I?"

She leans backward slightly to look up at me and shakes her head. "I only remember you pulling me from the river. Why?"

I give her a comforting smile. "Sometimes the forest can cause hallucinations. I wanted to be sure nothing still haunted you."

She gives me an identical smile back. "I don't believe in ghosts, Kai. I only believe in what I can see..."

I punctuate her sentence with a soft kiss. Taking her hand in mine, I make her rest her palm on my bare chest, sliding between my skin and my slightly open shirt. "Close your eyes," I tell her.

When she does, I press her hand harder over my petrified heart. In doing so, I give her my ultimate submission—full and untethered access to me. She can see all the memories I have of her that Amatisi stole. She can feel every moment of concern I've had for her and most importantly, she can feel how deeply I've fallen in love with her.

And worst of all—she can see my inevitable dread of losing her, and how powerless I am to stop it.

She wanted to see, and now she has.

She flinches away and I can see the tears well in her eyes as all of my emotions settle into hers in an overwhelming wave of fear and love.

The salty taste of her tears touches my tongue as I kiss her again. This time, there is no hesitation. There is no fear. There is only her and I and the space between us fading.

Without her even knowing, I've walked us to my bedroom. Too lost in our emotions, the back of her legs hit the bed and she falls onto her back as I hold myself over her. Her cheeks flush and the blue of her eyes grows smaller as her pupils grow larger.

My lips leave hers to trail down to her neck. I can feel her blood pulsing in her veins and I can smell the desire flowing through her body. I have not been known to lose control often in these centuries, but with her, I would let her destroy me.

I nip at her neck and then kiss down her body, lower and lower as I have before. I taste her and her back arches beautifully off the bed as a soft whimper escapes her lips. She tastes divine. I cannot decide if her core or her blood tastes better.

But then I realize that she's mine, and I have no reason nor desire to choose.

She gasps when one of my fangs nicks the inside of her thigh. When I slowly lick the cut, savoring the taste of her hot blood, her soft whimpers become desperate cries. The beautiful arch of her back becomes a roll of her hips, searching for more. Her fists tangled in the sheets become fists yanking on my hair to bring me closer. We become ravenous for each other and her taste is no longer enough. I need to feel her.

I continue to alternate between licking her core and the blood trickling down her thigh as I unlace my trousers. Freedom from the confines of my clothing only brings temporary relief. I swell and bob at the thought of feeling her heat around me. When I can no longer stand it, I crawl up the bed over her so I can see her face, flushed like a rose, and her chest panting for air.

I kiss her fiercely. Unable to control myself any longer, I tear at her nightgown until it's in tatters around her and I can see every inch of the toned dancer's body I've never had the privilege of marveling at until now.

A growl emanates from deep within my chest. "Oh, you are beautiful," I tell her, before kissing her again and allowing my fingers to dance over her center. She's so slick and warm. The smell of her blood and her sex mixing is intoxicating and driving me mad.

Her hand cradles my cheek and she quietly says my name. I meet her eyes to find that her cheeks have flushed an even darker shade of red.

Embarrassment, not desire.

"I've never..." she admits, looking down at the space between us and gulping slightly at the sight of me.

I mimic her actions and cradle her cheek with one hand while still circling her clit with the other. My lips ghost over hers and I breathe in every shuddering, nervous breath she takes. "I will be gentle. I promise. Just allow me this honor. *Please.*"

She nods. "On one condition."

"Tell me anything and it's yours," I whisper against her soft lips.

She delicately moves some strands of hair from her neck and turns her head to the side. "I want to feel everything."

I use my finger to move her chin to force her to face me again. Her heaving chest touches mine with every breath. The mere *thought* of her offering herself to willingly let me feed on her, to bring us both unimaginable pleasure...*oh Eternity forgive me for the way I will both defile and worship Adelasia this night.*

I can feel my fangs ache with need and my own blood begins rushing to my face. Now her scent is even stronger, her heartbeat even louder, her eyes even bluer.

The last time she saw me like this she was afraid, but I see no fear in her eyes. I see trust and I see....I see...

The hunger and desire overtake me and I slip into her slick core as my fangs pierce her neck. She cries softly at the intrusions, but then she arches into me, her legs wrap around me, she flutters intimately against me.

And in that moment, we are lost and consumed in a storm of blood and passion so unbelievably fierce that it links the chains of our very souls.

Twenty-Four
Adelasia

Brisk evening air dances over my body as I roll onto my back and sigh. I slept so well, with my dreams draped in…contentment.

When I stretch my arms, the curve of my neck aches and the memories come rushing back to me. The pleasure, the blood, the way Kaius worshiped the most sensitive parts of my body just as much as he worshiped the rest. I sit up with a satisfied groan and clutch the sheets to my chest as I rub the remaining sleep out of my eyes.

My back stiffens when I feel a cold finger trace down my spine. I turn and find Kaius still with me, his lower half covered by the same thin sheet and his naked torso on display. He is a beautiful man, with a thousand years of memories carved into his flesh. Scars where he's been stabbed with wooden stakes litter his chest and abdomen. I reach out to feel them. He does not seem ashamed of these scars as I am of mine. His fingers fold around mine and he squeezes them lightly.

"How are you feeling?" he asks, before his eyes lock on the marks on my neck. He gulps, but sheepishly smiles. "Forgive me...I lost myself in you. In your body. In your blood." The veins around his eyes darken as he remembers the taste. "You are invigorating." He pulls me easily on top of him, throwing the covers away so he can see all of me. My center quivers at his nearness.

"Can I ask you something?" I prompt. He nods. My cheeks reveal my embarrassment. "Is there a risk?" I ask, and then sigh as I elaborate. "Iphigenia told me that vampires can't reproduce. Was she telling the truth?"

His jaw hardens for a fraction of a moment, and then he nods. "*Male* vampires cannot reproduce. Female vampires can get pregnant by humans and even give birth, but the babes never survive infancy. They die slowly of starvation as they don't have fangs and their mothers do not produce milk."

"That's awful."

"Yes it is," he agrees. "But I am glad for it all the same. I would not wish this life on anyone—certainly not a child. If there were a way for me to enforce the cessation of transformations entirely, I would." He looks away from me and frowns. "To know that I am responsible for ruining so many lives with this curse is a burden I bear every day." His eyes meet mine and he pushes my messy hair away from my face to cup my cheeks. "Do you want to be a mother, Adelasia? Do not lie to me."

My mouth falls open slightly. "I...I'm not sure. I've never considered a future outside of dance. I know maybe it's not realistic to believe I could do it forever, but I did." I shrug. "I suppose that probably sounds pathetic to someone who has lived as many lifetimes as you."

"No," he says firmly. "It's not pathetic to be passionate about something you love. I envy you–I wish I had spent all these lifetimes being passionate about anything other than revenge. Perhaps I wouldn't have been so lonely."

"But you're not lonely anymore," I whisper, leaning in to press my lips to his. "You have me. Forever. I'm yours."

He furrows his brow as if in pain and turns his face from me slightly. I suddenly feel dejected as all the intimacy dissipates from the room. "You can't say things like that to me," he growls. "You know as well as I do that we do not have forever, nor could you possibly understand such a commitment."

Hoping to reason with him, I say, "Maybe you're right, I can't understand forever because I've only lived a small fraction of a life where you have lived many. But even if our forever is limited, isn't that enough? Aren't *I* enough?"

"Of course you are," he whines. He pulls me down slightly so our foreheads are pressed together. "But Adelasia, for me, forever without you is *so* much longer than forever with you."

"What if there was a way–"

"There's not."

"But–"

"There is not," he repeats.

I open my mouth to protest but shut it quickly. His eyes are closed as if in deep thought, and I can't help it when the next sentence falls from my lips.

"You could turn me into a vampire," I whisper.

Instantly, his body goes rigid and his eyes open with deep red fury. His loving embrace is gone and he practically shoves me off of his lap.

"That is out of the question!" he growls as he stands, using magic to clothe us both, me in my thin gown and him in his trousers. "I will not change you and I will hear no more suggestion of it."

"But–"

He approaches me with his unnatural speed and covers my mouth with his cold hand. He's furious–so furious he's shaking. "Do not dare to say those words again. Ever. The answer is no. It will always be no."

A bitterness seeps into my bones, an equal retaliation against his anger. As soon as he releases my mouth, I spit, "So I can give you my body, but surrendering my heart is too much?" I pull the invisible knife out of my chest and plunge it into his. "You're beginning to sound like Yekaterina."

"What did you just say to me?" he challenges, daring me to repeat myself. I scoff when he holds my neck, trying to threaten me, but his fingers only give the lightest of pressure. It's as if he knows I'm right, and he hates himself for it. "You don't understand—"

"I understand perfectly!" I shout. Kaius and I both stumble when the palace unexpectedly shudders at my voice, the delicate chandelier above the bed losing a few crystals as a result. I gulp and take a deep breath, and we resume scowling at each other. "I understand perfectly. Everything about you Kaius—you are predictable to a fault. I'm beginning to wonder if it was *you* who took advantage of the Priestesses all those years ago and that's why you were cursed. You treat my heart like a child's toy that they can drop and pick up as they please. Everything we do together is on your terms. I can't even trust a word you say unless you swear your life on it!"

He pauses, the color draining from his face as he drops to his knees. The energy shifts completely and he stares blankly at the room in front of him. He sags his head and shoulders in defeat. "I'm sorry. You're right. I'm sorry. But I cannot change you, Adelasia. Please don't ask it of me."

I close my eyes and sigh before kneeling next to him, running my fingers along his jaw. "Kai, are you afraid that I'll hate being immortal like you? Or are you scared that I won't?"

"Neither," he says, finally meeting my eyes. "It has nothing to do with immortality at all."

"Then what is it?"

"To break my curse, I have to kill you," he says as if it's an admission I haven't already come to face. "But to become a vampire, you would have to be killed as I drink from you." He cups my jaw in his large hands. "You will die either way, whether that's tomorrow or years from now, and I am not willing to risk your precious life in the hope that vampirism takes you instead of the Priestesses."

His words weigh heavy on my heart, because I can't comprehend how painful it has been for him to carry around that knowledge alone. I understand now how hard he has been trying to protect me from an uncertain fate.

"Are we truly destined for ruin?" I ask him, holding his hands to my heart. He leans his ear down to press against my chest, listening to the anxious beat as he tries to commit my life's symphony to memory.

He does not answer me with words. Instead, a sob trembles out of his throat.

No embrace nor consolation comforts us in the moonlight as we desperately cling to the moment.

For we both know we may not have another.

ARIEL N. ANDERSON

Twenty-Five
Adelasia

Kaius and I dread the next full moon. For ten days, it looms over us. He never leaves my side, and while he finds the courage to smile for me, I can see right through it. He's terrified, and truthfully, so am I.

Though I've witnessed death first-hand, the concept always seemed so far away. Death happened to others. Death happened around me. Certainly in the valley, death happened in front of me.

But never *to* me.

I've been fairly quiet in the days after Kaius touched my soul through the most intimate part of me. I think about my impending doom almost every moment of the day and night. Not his kiss nor his touch brings me any distraction, though he certainly tries.

It's become an unspoken understanding between us that we no longer look to the future. Instead, we focus on who we are now, not what we hope we can be.

Kaius also mourns his death. I can see it in his eyes. Not his physical death, but the true death of his mortality. While I don't doubt his passion for me, I fear he's struggling to cope. He's spent ten centuries longing to be a human again. He's giving that up for me. It's a selfless act of love, but one that devastates him all the same.

The gloomy overcast of a cold nighttime thunderstorm rages outside as Kaius slowly kisses up the scar on my back. As thunder cracks through the open windows, he bites down on the curve of my neck. I sigh with pleasure and my hips rise from the bed towards him. He smiles against the mark he just left, and a drop of blood falls from his fangs onto my chest as I turn over to face him.

I swipe the drop off my chest and place it on the tip of my tongue. He takes it from me with a passionate kiss as he enters me once more, intertwining our fingers together as he fills me over and over again with long, slow strokes.

Lightning strikes across the sky and thunder shakes the palace as we finish together. Kaius shifts to his back and I lie on my side next to him. I trace patterns on his chest and he watches my fingers as I watch his eyes slowly change from feral black to their normal savage red hue.

He looks stronger and more dangerous than I've ever seen him. I suppose him telling me that I was invigorating was more than just a compliment. I find myself wondering what it would be like to feed from the person you love.

But I would never admit that to him. His refusal to turn me into a vampire or even discuss it with me holds firm. It's almost like he can sense me thinking about it, and it puts him in a foul mood.

I fear it's the only way to save me. Save *us*.

And it's the only thing he will not give me.

The storm outside grows more violent and the sky grows darker with it. A dense gray fog seeps into the room, and Kaius uses his magic to shut the windows to keep it out. As the rain falls harder, I yawn and curl up next to him, seeking the warmth of a comforting embrace that he cannot give me with his skin alone.

With a wave of his fingers, a short nightgown appears to cover my naked body. I stifle a giggle and slightly shake my rear to show him that I've noticed the lack of fabric. All he does in return is smile wickedly and squeeze my thigh in a teasing warning.

"Behave. You know how hard it is for me to keep my hands off of you," he purrs.

I give him a subtle roll of my eyes and a slight upturn of my lips. "Your *hands* are not the problem," I whisper back, nipping at his ear as I do.

He chuckles and rolls over on top of me to use his breath and teeth to tickle my neck. "You don't seem to think it's a problem when—"

He pauses suddenly and wheezes in pain, as a human would when the wind gets knocked out of them.

"Kai?" I ask, holding his cheeks in my hands. He makes the noise again and sits back. I sit up with him and say his name again. He looks at me, and his mouth moves, but no words come out.

A painful groan leaves his throat instead, and his hands wrap around his neck.

When he lowers them, they're covered in blood.

Twenty-Six
Adelasia

"Kaius!" I shout frantically, scrambling to my knees on the bed. I hold my hands against his neck to try and stop the bleeding even though I know it's not helping.

Kai's body jolts several times, as if he's been struck, and seconds later, blood begins seeping out of invisible wounds on his chest.

Thunder and lightning once again rumble and crack across the sky. The bed under us fades into red mist and we now kneel on the cold ground of the throne room.

This is the work of Amatisi, it must be. Who else would make this much effort to terrorize us before showing themselves?

As black fog begins to cover the ground of the room, I find myself compelled to take the Bloodstone from Kaius. I lift it from his neck and place it around my own. It feels heavy with evil.

The assault on Kaius seems to have stopped. He's no longer paralyzed by pain. His wounds begin to slowly heal themselves. I raise my wrist to his mouth, compelling him to drink so he can heal faster.

But when I do, Kaius lets out another groan of pain and an invisible force lifts him from the ground, stretching his arms out to the side. A wooden post appears behind him, and a thick stake impales his chest, rendering him immobile. His hands grip the stake, attempting to free himself, but the wood has left him too weak. I touch his cheeks, and he slightly turns his head.

"Run," he chokes out.

"No," I answer. "I will not leave you."

The roof of the palace crumbles around us, drenching us in rain instantly. I shiver in the cold water that soaks into my bones.

And then, they appear.

All nine of the Priestesses stand in a line shoulder-to-shoulder across from Kaius and I. I stand between them and him, pulling the dagger from his boot and holding it out in front of me.

Amatisi's husky laugh fills my ears. "Stupid girl. Have you already forgotten your little blade cannot harm us?"

I swallow the fear in my throat, standing my ground. Amatisi takes a step forward, grabs my wrist, and forces me to cut along her own.

As she said, the blade does no harm to her. She releases my wrist.

I use the magic of the strange ruby around my neck to push her back. It only causes her to stumble slightly, only discernible because of the light fabric of her robe.

Though I cannot see her face, I can sense the challenge in her veiled gaze. She dares me to make a move, silently taunting the weak nature of my human soul.

A memory flashes across my mind. And then another.

The first, when Dravon threatened to kill me the last time the Priestesses were here. How she turned him into a griefclaw for threatening me, solidifying in my mind the value of my life to her—or at the very least, that my life be taken by the correct hands.

The second, when Kaius threw the dagger across the valley, and when it appeared again in front of us, it left a small cut on my finger when I touched it.

"The blade remains blunt until wielded by the cursebreaker."

My heart begins to race. All this time, I seem to have forgotten that it's not my life that Amatisi and the Priestesses care about. It's Yekaterina's, and only through my blood can she find life again. Fear and hope strike me at the same time. Is this the weakness in Kaius' curse that we haven't seen?

That the cursebreaker isn't him.

It's *me*.

"Amatisi," I say, the knife still clutched tightly in my hand. She turns to me with a hiss for daring to speak her name. "When Yekaterina is free, and Kaius is mortal again, what purpose will you have?"

"*Purpose?*" she repeats, then she scoffs. "You humans truly know nothing of the world you live in." She steps towards me and rips the Bloodstone from my neck. I instantly feel lighter without its dark aura weighing down on me. "Eternity gave her power to ten Priestesses. Without Yekaterina, Her will is defied. Her influence unbalanced. Her visage corrupted. With Yekaterina free, the Dark Goddess will enrich us once again, my Coven reigning over nature and magic as it was intended."

"And when Yekaterina is free, Kaius' debt to the Coven will be paid? He shall be free too?"

Amatisi cups my cheeks. "Oh, the mortal heart, so filled with hope," she mocks. "Even in the face of death you yearn for a man you cannot have. It is noble, truly."

"Answer the question," I demand.

"Kaius' debt will be satisfied when my sister returns," she says, and then tilts her head slightly as she adds, "*upon your death.*"

I take a deep breath. Amatisi is smart. She saw right through my attempt to change my fate. My eyes fill with burning tears as I look at Kaius, still hanging from the post and bleeding. I step toward him and rise onto my toes to kiss the underside of his chin.

My touch seems to wake him from his daze and his eyes slightly open to focus on me.

"Adelasia..."

I cup his cheek and the tears begin to fall from my eyes. "Will you make me a promise, Kaius?"

"Anything..." he whispers out painfully, blood dripping from his mouth.

"Promise me that you'll live the full life you've always wanted. Promise me I won't die in vain."

The mention of my death seems to slightly pull him from his delirium and he raises his head. His eyes trace my face and reveal confusion.

I take a shuddering breath and turn the blade to face my stomach. "Promise me..." I beg quietly. His body begins to twitch and move awkwardly as he attempts to free himself from the post.

"Adelasia, don't!" he shouts as he falls to the ground and reaches for me.

A small whimper escapes my lips. Time feels frozen at first—everything seems to stop moving. I let out a humorless laugh at the odd pressure in my abdomen.

Only when my eyes meet Kai's again, because I cannot bear to look, I pull the blade free from my body and drop it at my side.

Twenty-Seven
Kaius

Numbness overtakes my body at what Adelasia has done.

I watch the dagger clatter to the ground, splattering drops of her blood on the floor.

She looks at me with a distant gaze, and huffs as if she can't believe it herself. As if the regret settles into her and she realizes I wasn't worth it after all.

My own injuries and pain disappear with the numbness, and the world begins to move again. Her body falls limp and I barely catch her before her knees hit the marble. I hold her face tenderly in my hands, but she does not focus on me. Her hand clutches her stomach, blood beginning to spill over the top of her fingers.

She hisses and jerks away from me to curl on her side in the fetal position. A painful moan escapes on an exhale of her breath. The air grows colder around her when a black mist begins to spill out of her stomach along with her blood, followed by a loud *crack*.

Adelasia whimpers, and another loud crack follows. Then another. And another. She rolls slightly to lie more on her stomach, her chest heaving harshly between the pain.

With one more crack, a pool of blood seeps through the delicate fabric of her beige gown. Slowly, the scar down the length of her back morphs into the color of fresh blood, and from the blood, a hand pushes through her skin in a pool of black mist. The long fingernails grip her skin and push through her spine, the mist flowing upward and outward until landing with a soft thud on the marble.

This is Yekaterina's soul escaping from Adelasia's, and only through her death will the Priestess return to this plane.

Adelasia's time is limited, but without my Bloodstone, what can I do to help? I couldn't even save her from a werewolf bite without that dark magic. How could I possibly hope to save her from this certain fate without it?

"Kai..."

I hold her to my chest and wipe the tears from her eyes. I've never seen them so lifeless. The vivid royal blue I've always been so fond of has faded into a vacant gray. Her lips have gone purple and her skin a ghastly white.

"Kai..." she chokes out again. "Change me."

My lips quiver and I can't help but deny her. "I can't." I shake my head. "I can't Adelasia. I won't do that to you. I won't take your life from you."

"I'm dying anyway."

I shake my head and squeeze her gently even tighter to my chest. "What if you don't come back to me?"

She does her best to give me a reassuring smile through her tears, but I can see the emotion stuck in her throat, bubbling up and making her lip quiver. She doesn't know the answer, but I do.

If she doesn't come back, then I shall chase her into the afterlife when the sun rises.

She notices when I crumble, ready to risk everything on the minuscule chance that it could save her. "Will it hurt?" she asks quietly.

I tenderly brush her hair away from her neck to comfort her. "No. No, it won't hurt. I promise."

I close my eyes and press my fangs through the delicate skin of her neck. She tenses up for a second before she begins to fall limp into my arms as the euphoria takes her. It masks her pain and her fear.

Her blood does not bring me pleasure. Not this time. Not when I'm stealing her precious life from her. I want to stop. I find myself fighting the urge to gag, fighting the urge I have to stop drinking from her. I don't want her to die by my hand, even if she's already doomed.

I've already ruined her life. I don't want to be the one to end it, too. As she begins to fall limp from the loss of blood, her soft breath fans across my neck on the opposite side.

"I love you, Kaius. I'm sorry I didn't tell you sooner."

My brow furrows and ice shoots through my heart as I softly hold her head. I let her take one last peaceful intake of breath before I quickly and seamlessly jerk her neck.

With a soft click, she goes fully limp and still in my arms. I taste my salty tears as I remove my teeth from her neck and the devastation hits me all at once.

I tenderly kiss her temple. "I love you too."

A hand grabs me by the back of my head, twisting into my hair and pulling it backward.

"What have you done?!" Amatisi yells into my face, her veil billowing slightly from her words getting caught on her breath.

Yekaterina's summoning mist has begun to crackle like a storm cloud. Black lightning flashes through the air above us. Amatisi lets out an exasperated sound somewhere between a shout and a growl. The ground shakes below us through her fury. Her hand flicks to her side, pulling Adelasia's still body out of my grip. Amatisi holds me by the front of my jacket.

I grit my teeth, no longer trying to hide my sorrow. My eyes leak tears freely. I have nothing now. No mortality. No Adelasia.

What else could I possibly lose?

"There is no hell deep enough for you, Kaius Voroninov. The next time you look upon me, my crown will be made from the bones of your lover."

Amatisi clutches her fist, and like a candle snuffed out from the wind, the Priestesses are gone, taking Adelasia's body with them.

The only sounds that can be heard through the valley are my wails, drowned out by the harsh sprinkle of a heavy rain.

Twenty-Eight
Adelasia

Cold. That's the first thing I notice, but I've grown used to it by now, the way my toes and fingers never quite find a comfortable temperature anymore.

Then, I hear the soft lap of waves. Not as intense as the ocean, more like the edge of a lake, gently disturbed after a nighttime swim.

I open my eyes and find myself half-submerged in a pool of black water. My spine tingles uncomfortably. The last time I was in black water, I nearly drowned.

But this time...this time I'm already dead.

I pull myself to my knees and brush the strands of hair stuck to my face away from my cheeks before taking in my surroundings.

I sit on a small island in the center of a black lake. The water is eerily still and the ground below me is chilly and lifeless. A statue stands tall before me of a veiled woman. The stone is a deep black adorned with golden details. Her veils and robes sit luxurious on her frame and a black crystal crown proudly gleams atop her head. Golden wings protrude from her back, seeming to both absorb and reflect all light within this strange place.

You shall be punished...

An eerie voice echoes in the space around me.

You shall be punished...

You shall be punished...

You. Shall. Perish!

I gasp as a forceful grip pulls my head back. It's a Priestess, but this one I do not know. Her robes are different from the others. Much more worn and decayed.

Her headdress is broken too, but stabbed through one of the spikes on the ornate golden crown is an eye.

"Yekaterina..."

"You dare speak my name?!" she challenges, but then her voice softens. "How does it feel? To be free of your worldly, human burdens? To stand in the presence of our

Dark Goddess?" She gestures to the statue. "She is beautiful, isn't she?" She kneels and brings her long, slender fingers to her face in prayer. "Oh blessed be, Eternity. How long it's been since I've felt your shadowy grace."

She kisses the feet of the statue, then stands to face me. "Bow," she commands, and Yekaterina's magic forces me to my knees. She stands between the statue and me, her robes billowing in a sudden wind.

I give her a stern look as I stare through her veil, trying to meet her eyes. "Where am I?"

"This is the Well of Eternity. The birthplace of magic and the temple of our Dark Lady."

"Why am I here?" I ask. "Your soul has been returned to your sisters and I am dead. What more could you need from me?"

"I simply wanted to have a conversation with the sweet human that stole my Kaius' heart. How lovely it was to watch you resist each other for so long. Oh, and the theatrics of declaring your love for him as you faced your death. *Delicious.*" She sarcastically giggles. "And of course, I can't forget the pleasure. I wonder who it was he thought about while he was lost in it. I'm willing to bet I slipped into his mind at least once."

I stand, and Yekaterina removes her veil from her head so she truly has to look me in the eye. Her broken crown falls with the fabric, and I drink in the face of the woman who has caused Kaius so much misery.

She is beautiful, no doubt. A perfect set of teeth inside a sultry smile. Long, white hair neatly arranged in a bun. Her deep red eyes soak into mine.

I can suddenly understand so clearly why Kaius hates himself. She cursed him to look like the monster that stole his life from him. A reflection of her. A constant reminder of the person he loathes the most.

"What did he ever do to deserve what you did except devote himself to you?"

"Devotion is just a fool's word for desperation."

I scoff. "Is that what you are then? Desperate for Eternity's approval? So devoted to proving how cruel you can be to gain her favor?"

She smacks me. "Do not dare to tell me who I am."

She tries to push me into the water, and I trip over the discarded crown in the dirt. The upper half of my body lands in the water.

"You should be thanking me!" she boasts. "If I hadn't given him this *gift* of immortality, you would have never met him, and your useless human heart wouldn't have tasted the beauty of Eternity's magic."

"I don't care about Eternity. I just want him."

She smiles down at me, pressing her foot into my back, shoving my head and cheek into the stale mud on the lake's edge.

"I was his first love, and he shall love me again. He will forget about you in another thousand years, I'm certain."

Her words give me pause. My death was supposed to free him from his curse, and now she reveals that she never had any intentions of making him human again.

I grow furious at her, pushing her leg from me and grabbing her broken headdress as I grip her long hair. I press the tip of the crown into her throat.

"Send me back to him," I demand.

She snickers. "Or what?" She presses her neck further into the spiked headdress, enough to make her bleed, but she shows no sign of pain. "You cannot kill me."

"For now," I concede, dropping my hand to the side. "But who is to say I won't make you suffer anyway?"

I raise my hand to her face, and with bated breath, I reach into her eye socket and pull out her left eye, just as she stole Kaius' mother's. It separates from her skull with a pop, and as she screams in pain, I steal the Bloodstone from her chest, too. A dark mist gathers on the small island, and the other Nine Priestesses appear before us. Eight of them tend to their wounded sister, crying on her knees.

Amatisi though, comes straight to me. She attempts to take the stone from around my neck, but I back further into the dark water.

"Give it to me!" she roars, her demonic voice resonating through the sky.

A cyclone begins to form above the small island, the wind making both of us lose our balance. A red streak of lightning strikes Eternity's statue, causing the golden elements to shine a bright white. The ground begins to shake and the wind howls louder.

And then, a moment of serene silence before being broken by another crack of lightning that resonates from the statue directly to the Bloodstone around my neck.

The force knocks me into the water, and I find myself unable to breathe in the intense weight of the Well. I sink further and further, watching red lightning streak in the sky far above me until I'm so deep I can no longer see.

You shall be punished...

You shall be punished...

You. Shall. Perish!

That voice fills my mind again, and I see a black thread appear above my head, sinking with me like a delicate locket lost at sea. It glows with a red aura, appearing to almost be painted in the water. I reach for it, and the very tip of my finger brushes against it.

It begins to consume me, wrapping my arms first, and then my chest and legs until I am a glowing void floating in an unforgiving black lake.

"Kaius..." I say, bubbles escaping my mouth.

And then, he's there. In the distance. Trapped behind a wall of water. I can see him on his knees, crying in the ruins of the Obsidian Palace.

"Kaius!" I say again, but he does not hear me.

I attempt to swim closer, reaching for him through the water.

Something grabs my shoulder from behind and I turn, the water disappearing at the same time. I cough what's left of it out, and another robed figure sits before me. It breathes heavily as I do.

"Who are you?" I ask. But I receive no answer. Hanging from her neck is a bloodstone, and clutched in her hand is an eyeball with a red iris. I look down to see that clutched in my own hand is the same eye, and around my own neck is the same chain.

I blink rapidly and then turn to look at Kaius, still distraught behind whatever plane of existence separates us.

"Please," I beg quietly to the figure in front of me. "I want to go back to him. I love him."

You were created for things greater than love...

Resurrection is forbidden...

You shall be punished.

You shall be punished.

I take a deep breath and look behind me one more time.

My Kaius, my bloodking, my heart, all alone in the world again. I would face any punishment to keep him from feeling that way. I would face any punishment for *us*.

You shall be punished.

You shall be punished.

I ignore the words in my head, and with tightly shut eyes, I jump towards Kaius through the wall separating us.

He. Shall. Perish!

Twenty-Nine
Kaius

I thought I knew what loneliness felt like.

It feels like I've lost half of myself...no, more than that. I have nothing left at all. Both halves of my soul were taken from me when she died.

And I am the one that killed her.

She did not come back to me. Our last moments together were marred by the false hope that she would return as a vampire–the false hope that we could cheat fate.

So she is gone, and I am to blame.

And, as cruelty would have it, I am still a vampire, and so she died for nothing.

My love. My sweet agony. My heart. My poison. My soul. My reason.

Gone.

There is nothing left for me here. Nothing that would ease this suffering and nothing that would bring me happiness. The only thing I have left to do is wait until the sun is high enough to caress my skin.

This time, I shall let it burn.

The walls of my broken palace leave nothing in the shadows as the sun begins to rise. The soft oranges dance across the sky, but I see no vibrancy in the color. Though my eyes can see the different hues, my heart sees only black and white.

When the sun crests over the valley, I turn my head away from the bright light. I slowly open the front of my tunic to expose more of my chest to the sun and I wait for the bitter, searing sting of the light piercing my skin.

A soft laugh comes from behind me. "I thought you were jealous of the sun, but from where I'm sitting, it looks to me like you wish to seduce it."

My head twitches at her voice. A twisted illusion, surely, left behind by the Priestesses to torture me. I open my eyes, for the sun does not burn, and notice there's a dark ward surrounding the palace, blocking the sunlight from touching me.

My hand touches my chest in confusion, and I stand to reach through the ward, believing that I'm being deceived.

As my fingers touch the magic, I'm pulled backward, landing on my back in front of the steps that led to my throne.

I open my eyes. From my position on my back and my head nearly upside down resting on a rock, I see a long velvet train in a deep oxblood color.

Sitting on the ruins of what used to be my throne, is a woman wearing a golden headdress adorned with red jewels that hum a dark energy. She motions a finger to the side and the veil covering her face disappears into a fine mist. She smiles at me, her teeth a beautiful pearly white with two short but sharp fangs. She licks them and raises her chin a bit.

Then, my eyes meet hers. Stunningly vibrant and blue just like I remember them, framed by dark brows and thick lashes.

"Adelasia?" I whisper, still believing I'm in an illusion. I flip over and sit back on my knees. My mouth opens slightly in disbelief. Stabbed through one of the spikes on her head is a red eye.

I approach her with my supernatural speed, arms open and ready to embrace her, but she stops me with a foot to my chest. I wrap my hand around the sole and squeeze to prove she's real.

With a dead, emotionless face, she quietly says, "Kneel."

"Adelasia—"

Black magic wraps around my mouth to cut off her name, and she waves her black-tipped finger at me as if I'm a petulant child.

"Kneel, Kaius Voroninov, before your queen."

She releases me and I do as she says, my mouth still agape in confusion.

"Good little crow," she purrs, leaning forward to take my chin in her hands. "But we need to work on your listening skills."

Something seems…off about her. The theatrics, the voice, the cruelty in her tone. But under all of that, she is still my Adelasia.

"Here's your first lesson," she says, and then slowly, without us breaking eye contact, she places one foot on my shoulder and spreads the other slightly before pressing me forward with her heel. "I don't ask twice. Surely you're familiar with that concept?"

She leans back once again, raises her chin, and I smile at my new Queen.

And she is absolutely, stunningly *wicked*.

Keep reading for chapter one of

Book Two: Queen of the Wicked.

One
Adelasia

It's been all but three days since I've become…

Well, I'm not sure. No longer a human, but not quite a vampire.

My senses are sharper, but I do not burn in the sunlight. I have fangs and crave blood, but I cannot drink human blood. Getting used to my newfound strength has been a challenge, for I bend and warp and break almost everything I touch.

It gives me…a sense of sadness, to know that Kaius had to use such care when touching me before. He never once left a bruise on me. The restraint he must have shown is remarkable.

The only physical indications of any change in me are the tips of my fingers, which have turned a deep black color as if frostbitten. I can still function and feel with them, so my best assumption is that it was the first part of my human body to "*die*" before I forced my own resurrection.

But more than that...I can feel something inside me has shifted too, yet I can't describe it, nor can I tell if that change is for better or worse.

It's strange, living in what feels like a body that does not belong to me.

Perhaps this is what I truly am, and the difference I feel is the lack of Yekaterina's soul intertwined with mine. Perhaps this is what freedom feels like.

It's dusk.

In the time since Saddiq's passing, I have never broken my promise to him. I visit him every day. His shrine was once flourishing with flora and bright green fauna, but since my resurrection, it's degraded into weeds and dead plants. All the work I put in vanished with my death, as if the foliage here knew of my demise.

And ever since that change, I can't seem to make any of the flowers bloom again. The shrine sits lifeless— and I wonder if this is Saddiq punishing me for attempting to become one of the demons he spent his life hunting.

As if he needed another reason to hate me.

I sigh as I look up at the shrine, and just as the dusk turns into the night, I begin to dance in front of it. No shoes, no precision, no expectations. I simply let the gentle whoosh of a sudden wind carry my body into expressive shapes.

The wind grows louder and as I come out of a turn, I pause, looking at the space around me. The wind begins to beat in a rhythmic pattern.

Whoosh...whoosh...whoosh. Almost like a heartbeat.

Then, it stops, and I hear a set of footsteps behind me. I tense and turn quickly. In my hand, a sharp knife appears at the throat of the intruder.

I blink rapidly, confused as to how I did that without realizing I could, and then meet the peculiar gray irises of a tall, dark-haired man. Expanding behind him in a brilliant flash of white are massive feathered wings.

Still cautious, the man notices my stance and holds his hands up in surrender.

"My apologies for scaring you," he says softly. His voice is a sultry, smoky baritone–almost a purr.

I continue to stare at him as if in a trance. I've seen him before—his eyes are so painfully familiar to me...as if I'm staring at an old friend.

Suddenly, I realize it's not the eyes themselves, but the color of them. Their owner is an aloof creature that I just now realize I haven't seen in days.

I slightly lower my knife and furrow my brow. "Cassius?" I ask inquisitively.

"Not quite," he answers. He gives me a smile that is devilish and oh-so-handsome. Something about the gesture brings an unconscious blush to my cheeks. My skin suddenly feels hot and I have the urge to rip off my gown.

I rub my neck, suddenly very uncomfortable.

What is happening to me? Why do I feel...

"Who are you?" I demand through the racing thoughts in my head. Thoughts of touching and being touched. Thoughts of whimpering and sighing. My back hits the cold outer wall of the Obsidian Palace and relief washes through me at the cold marble cooling my molten skin.

The man reaches for my other hand and brings it to his lips. A gasp escapes my throat. I tug my hand free from his.

Through my haze, I say, "I've seen you before."

He raises a brow. A gentle tip of one of his wings traces the underside of my jaw while the other just barely brushes my calf. I begin to breathe heavier and feel my cheeks grow warmer. "Have you?" he asks.

"In...in a dream."

One of his hands rests on the marble above my head and he leans into me, sinfully whispering his name across my shoulder.

"*Rowan*. Remember that name, darling. I sense I will be occupying more than just your dreams soon."

Pronunciation Guide

Kaius Voroninov: Kie-us Vore-on-in-ovh

Adelasia LeMasters: Add-eh-lay-zhuh Leh-mass-turs

Dravon: Drah-vunn

Cassius: Cass-ee-us

Iphigenia: If-eh-jen-eye-uh

Saddiq al-Abadi: Sad-eek al-ah-bah-dee

Yekaterina: Yeh-cat-er-ee-nah

Amatisi: Am-ah-tee-see

Zecate: Zek-ah-tee

Gaia: Guy-ah

Octavia: Oct-ay-vee-uh

Marcella: Mar-cell-ah

Nephele: Neh-fell

Selene: Sell-eene

Viseria: Vis-air-ee-ah

Nyx: Nix

Avrusa: Av-roo-sah

Cambouri (Desert): Cam-boar-ee

Acknowledgements

Thank you to Kristen, whose snakes are the namesakes of seven of the nine Priestesses. Thank you to Shelby, who is my closest and most trusted friend in this industry.

To my mother and my husband, whose support and love is what gets me up in the morning. To my PA Samantha for helping me through this crazy, rewarding life.

To the American Foundation for Suicide Prevention and their representatives for taking the time to learn my story and the impact it's had on the romance community. I am proud to continue to use my platform and books to support your cause.

To JA. Because watching you thrive after what you've been through has made me proud to call you a friend. All of my love and wishes of success are with you, always.

To RE and JC, who are not afraid to kick me in the ass when it's needed. While my writing career was never meant to be something I did long term, the two of you always look out for it. I hope every author finds the support and friendship that I've found in you.

And finally, but maybe most importantly, to my readers. Without you, I would be nothing. While I may not always have the time to respond to your messages, know that I see them and cherish them. Thank you for giving me the most incredible experiences of my life.

Made in the USA
Coppell, TX
29 January 2026

70277199R00164